CASTLE
OF
SHADOWS

A Story about Karensa

Jean Cullop

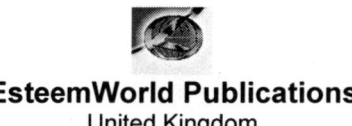

EsteemWorld Publications
United Kingdom

CASTLE OF SHADOWS

Copyright © 2010 By Jean Cullop

ISBN: 978-1-907011-07-8

First Published 2001 in the United Kingdom, by
Scripture Union

Now Re-published in the United Kingdom, by
EsteemWorld Publications

British Library Cataloguing In Publication Data
A Record of this Publication is available from the
British Library.

For further information or permission, address:
EsteemWorld Publications
United Kingdom.
E-mail: info@esteemworldpublications.com
www.esteemworldpublications.com

By the same Author

Where Dolphins Race with Rainbows
Children of the Second Morning
Silver Serpent, Golden Sword
Average Alex Brown

Printed in Great Britain for EsteemWorld Publications

Contents

The Lost Kingdom

As far away as yesterday there is an island called Karensa, where dolphins race with rainbows and animals walk freely in the Dark Forest, and broken hearts are healed.

The people of Karensa live and speak in the ways of ancient times and were ruled by their King with perfect love and justice until one day, everything changed.

Bellum, a Lord of the Palace, disobeyed the King. This brought fear and death to the island. Bellum was forced to leave the Royal Palace for ever and people were no longer allowed to approach the King.

Lord Bellum then built a castle from where he planned to one day rule Karensa. Many people followed him and believed the false promises he made.

But this King still loved his people more than they would ever know. To save them from punishment and to remove death from Karensa, he sent his own son, Salvis, to die in their place.

Doing this meant that the King's own heart would be broken.

Salvis obeyed his father, the King, and at the very same moment he gave his life, all the people who had been held captive in Bellum's castle were set free.

Defeat for Salvis became victory for the people.

Salvis did not deserve to die and because the King's justice is perfect, he now lives again in the Royal Palace. All those who put their trust in him are forgiven and receive the King's power.

So it will be on Karensa until the day when Salvis rides out to claim back the Lost Kingdom.

Chapter 1

The Meadow of Flowers

Morwen was paddling. She had rolled up the legs of her trousers and she was splashing in the ice cold water of the stream.

It was the warmest day she could ever remember in the whole of her twelve years. She had turned up the sleeves of her tunic so that her freckled arms were bare. Her red-gold hair was braided and wound around her head to keep her neck cool.

"Come in, Petroc!" she called to her brother, screwing up her light green eyes against the sun. "The water is so cold! It will cool you down."

Thirteen-year-old Petroc shook his head. He was sitting comfortably in a shady spot he had found, and he replied that he was too lazy to move. The water did look good. The clear stream chattered happily through the Meadow of Flowers from the Dark Forest into the very heart of Karensa.

The truth was Petroc was embarrassed. For many months, all through the war, his loyalty to the King had kept him a prisoner in Bellum's evil stronghold, forced to work for the cruel Lord Carrik, Bellum's highest servant and also the King's enemy. His captivity had left him weak and thin, so although he was still tall, the rest of him had become thin and wasted. He had no intention of revealing his white, spindly legs to Morwen or to anyone else.

So he sat where he was, hot and tired, and continued to look out towards the sea.

Morwen looked at him and sighed inwardly. She knew how unhappy her brother was, and she felt guilty that she could not share his sadness, but today the world felt good. The sky was blue and the sun was hot and the grass was strewn with wild flowers of every colour. Their scent was heavy on the breeze.

She splashed her way through the crystal clear water, up and down the stream until at last she grew tired and sat down by Petroc's side.

"You seem so sad," she ventured. "Is it because Lord Salvis has returned to the Royal Palace?"

"Salvis?" Petroc's voice rose angrily. "No, not Salvis!"

"Then it must be because Luke and Rosie have gone home."

Petroc's face was expressionless. He had the same red hair and green eyes as his sister but where she bubbled with life, his eyes were dull and his pale, drawn face seemed defeated and without purpose.

As usual, Morwen had been right. Petroc was thinking of their two friends, Luke and Rosie, who had been visitors from the world beyond the mist that surrounded the island of Karensa. *

He did miss them. His one thought during all those months when he had been forced to live in Bellum's stronghold, was to escape and rejoin his family and friends. It was the only thing that had given him hope when he felt all else was hopeless. He and Luke had become closer than brothers, in spite of their different worlds, or maybe because of them? Petroc had never known anyone so well as Luke.

---

* *This story is told in Where Dolphins Race with Rainbows*

When at last Petroc was set free, Salvis had decided that it was time for Luke and Rosie to go home.

Morwen placed her hand over her brother's hand, her hand freckled and brown, his wasted and pale. Her hand was cool from the stream.

"I miss them too, brother," she said gently. "Especially... especially Luke... Luke was special to me, but... they had to go home... Their world is not our world..."

"It has been two days since they left. Do you think they are home yet?"

"Of course they are! The dolphins who guided them have returned and are playing in the deep waters off the bay. Oh, Petroc I know we shall see them again one day, and... and... I miss Lord Salvis too... I do not think there was ever anyone like him, ever before."

"Salvis, Salvis; that is all I hear! What do you know, Morwen? You know nothing! You cannot even begin to imagine what Bellum is really like! Do you think it was easy, being made to serve him? And what did Salvis do? Nothing at all! He didn't even put up a fight!"

"When he died you were set free."

"He didn't die! How could he have really died? He was standing talking to us on the beach a few days later!"

By now tears were trickling down Morwen's face.

"He did die, Petroc. You know it. You saw it happen," she sobbed.

"Then it must have been a trick."

"You know it was not. You know it was real. Oh, Petroc, you have changed! Once you would never have spoken so."

Petroc looked away from her. Even in his present mood he was sorry to have made her cry.

And she was right, but once there had been no war on Karensa. Once the King had ruled with perfect justice and taken care of all his people's problems.

Once it had been right for Petroc to obey his father, Tobias, but now Tobias was dead; killed by Carrik, their landlord, whom Petroc had been forced to serve.

Once... once he and Morwen had been happy, just simple farm children; loved and cared for. Now their farm was burnt to the ground.

Once he'd had plenty to eat. He had never known hunger. Now he had endured months of near starvation.

Once, the King's servants had been pleased to serve a King who ruled with perfect justice. Now, Lord Bellum had disobeyed that King and so he had been thrown out of the Royal Palace, taking a third of the King's servants with him.

Within hours of Bellum's disobedience, fear and death had come to the island of Karensa, until at last the King had sent his son, Salvis, to stand against Bellum. Salvis had lost his life and at that very moment, the prisoners in Bellum's castle, including Petroc, had been set free.

Now the war was over but things would never be quite the same as they were before.

From the corner of his eye, across the shallow Meadow of Flowers, Petroc could see the dark outline of Bellum's stronghold where the King's enemy still lived and ruled.

"Brother, do you realise," Morwen said suddenly, "It was at this very spot that Lord Salvis was taken prisoner on the night he died?"

"Let himself be taken, you mean. Why didn't he fight? He could easily have defeated Bellum. He had an army at his side; all those who stayed loyal to the King."

"That was not the way it had to be. Oh Petroc, it is because you never really got to know him. You did not have time. While you were... were captured, Lord Salvis lived with us, all through the Time of Snows. If only you could have known him for yourself! He had this sort of peaceful feeling. Even when he knew he was going to die he still had that peace. It feels as though he left some of it behind with his friends when he died."

Abruptly, Petroc stood up and turned his back on her. As he turned his back, he closed his heart.

Morwen rolled down the legs of her trousers and eased her feet into her soft boots. It seemed wrong that anyone should be sad on such a day. The Time of Plenty was too short on Karensa. Soon enough the Time of Gathering would be here, only this year they had no harvest to gather; for they had no farm any more. Not for the first time Morwen wondered what their future would be.

They were still living in a cave house at the Bay of Dolphins, but they could not stay there for ever. She supposed decisions would soon have to be made about their future. She pushed such thoughts right from her mind. Petroc was unhappy. She was sad because she missed Luke and Rosie and Lord Salvis.

Yet she was not going to let anything spoil such a perfect day.

Chapter 2

Words of Ancient Days

From the highest window of the Royal Palace, the King and his son could see over the entire kingdom of Karensa.

The King bowed to his son, and as he moved his head, the jewels in his crown reflected bright colours on his royal robes of purple and gold.

His son's head was bare, and he was dressed in a simple grey tunic and loose fitting trousers, but the power surrounding him revealed that he was indeed the son of a great king and that his peasant clothes meant nothing.

Above them, the golden turrets and silver pennants of the Palace shimmered; below them, the island of Karensa basked peacefully in the morning sunshine. The war was over. Peace was being proclaimed throughout the land.

"Welcome home, Salvis," said the King. "My son, I am well pleased. You were obedient to my word, even to death."

Salvis inclined his head so that his light brown hair fell across his face.

"Father, you know that it was for this purpose that I was born," he said simply.

"Ah yes, my son, but I did not force you to obey me. This was your decision. You could have refused."

"Then the people would never have been able to enter the Royal Palace again, for that is what your word decreed."

"Salvis, my word is higher than all things, even my own desires. When my people turned away from me, I could no longer allow them inside the Royal Palace walls because their disobedience would have put an end to my perfect justice. You alone were obedient and you were willing to die in their place. You took the punishment that should have been theirs. You died instead of them, although you were innocent of any crime. Now I give you back your life for ever and you shall receive the highest honour."

"So the war is ended, Father?"

The King sighed. "No, it is not ended, Salvis. Our enemy Bellum still lives in his castle on the far side of the Dark Forest, just beyond the Meadow of Flowers. His castle is fast becoming a mighty stronghold. Many will listen to Bellum. The war has only just begun."

The King and Salvis stood silently considering these things, for they loved the people of Karensa with a love that went beyond sacrifice.

They were joined by the King's most loyal and faithful servant, Veritan, Lord of the Palace. He was almost as splendid as the King, with a jewelled circlet over his long, silver hair, and precious gems shining from his belt and from the hilt of his golden sword.

"All seems well, Lord King."

Once again the King sighed, an eternal sigh for all the world's deep sorrows.

"There is much to accomplish before Bellum is finally defeated and Karensa is ours once more. Even today, Veritan, I am sending you out with work to do."

"Anything, Lord King... but..." Veritan hesitated.

"Speak your mind," commanded the King. "You need have no fear of me, Veritan. You have been faithful to me in all things."

"It is only... Lord King... why not be done with Bellum now, once and for ever? Why not simply end his power?"

The King looked down across the sunlit island and beyond to where the mist obscured the horizon. Karensa was always surrounded by this mist. It rarely cleared.

The King's face became thoughtful and sad.

"Bellum... Bellum once loved me," he said at last, choosing his words with great care. "Remember the music he made for us in the time before the war? Such music helped my people worship me, but then... yet that is not the reason... There are many people on Karensa who wish to come into the Royal Palace and who would love the old laws to return. They have the right to choose between Bellum and my justice."

"But Lord King... you are all powerful, and Salvis, too has your power, the very power of creation. Bellum is nothing. He turned your people against you. He is a liar... a deceiver... a serpent... nothing at all..."

"Bellum has all the power my people are willing to give him. No less; no more. I will not permit anyone to take authority above my word. One day Salvis will cast Bellum from Karensa, never to return. Until then the battle goes on. Now let us rejoice as we welcome my son home."

At the far end of the Great Hall, on a high platform were three marble thrones. On both sides of the hall the King's servants were assembled, each one dressed in shining white. The pure brightness of their robes contrasted with the many coloured banners hanging from each stone pillar. The hall was lit by a strange

13

silver light which transformed the marble floor into a sea of moving colours.

The King led the way towards the thrones and as he did so, Salvis changed. His robes became dazzling white, and as he walked further and further towards the thrones, his face began to shine with the radiance of a thousand suns, and to reflect the quiet peace of a thousand moons. Even in his brilliance, all servants who had true hearts could look upon Salvis without fear, for although his eyes flashed fire, it was a fire born of the greatest love in all creation.

The King commanded Salvis to kneel and he placed a crown on his son's head, a crown that sent rays of light in every direction so that it was never still.

Then at last Salvis took his place at the right hand of the King. A mighty shout of joy and triumph arose as each servant began to praise the King in words older than time and sweeter than tomorrow's dawn, secret words of ancient days, words of power and great beauty, never before spoken and now carved into eternity.

The King and Salvis took their seats, and with them, the presence of an unseen lord fell upon the third throne. All three thrones, although separate were one, as they always had been and as they always would be. The Three were One and yet were Three. It was the Deep Secret of Creation.

The King gave a loud cry, a heart cry full of love and victory, a cry that resounded through the entire universe.

"Now, my son who was dead is alive again! Now my people can come to me once more! Now, Salvis you wear your royal robes. You made yourself lower than the least of my people. You accepted the worst that Bellum could do and did not once falter or turn away from me or the work I had given to you. One day you will judge the people of Karensa and from now onward all those who trust in you will be welcomed into the Royal Palace. Meanwhile, let the battle continue. Salvis has already won the final victory, but the spoils of war have yet to be divided. Now my people must choose whom they will follow, and Bellum will try everything in his power to keep them from coming to me, for he desires only that they should worship him, and he is a cunning adversary. My friends, this is where the real conflict starts."

Veritan lifted high the golden sword of truth and a great and mighty call to arms resounded around the Hall and was carried to the ends of the Earth.

Chapter 3

A Fallen Crown

As Morwen and Petroc sat in the sun by the stream, there was a sudden movement over by the edge of the Dark Forest.

Morwen stood up, shading her green eyes against the sun.

"Petroc, see over there, butterflies, hundreds of them!"

Coming towards them across the Meadow of Flowers, was a beautiful coloured cloud, a cloud made from fluttering wings that shimmered in the heat haze, pink and blue, purple and white, yellow, red and gold.

The cloud came nearer and to Morwen's delight, the butterflies flew all around them until they were completely hidden in the moving cloud.

Butterfly wings brushed their cheeks, their lips, their eyes, their hands. They were soft as gossamer.

"Listen Petroc, listen to their song!"

Her brother could hear nothing. He stood there with the lovely creatures fluttering all around him and he might have been made of stone.

"Butterflies do not sing, Morwen," he said flatly.

"They do! They do! They make music with their wings! I never heard such a sound! Like the breath of bells, thousands and thousands of little bells. But so sad, such sad music!"

Still Petroc heard nothing. As the butterflies moved on across the Meadow of Flowers, Morwen became agitated.

"Petroc, we must stop them. They are on their way to Bellum's stronghold. We must not let them go there!"

In desperation she began to call, "Butterflies, butterflies, come back!"

The butterflies, as if drawn by a great magnet, were heading straight towards the one place where they should not go.

Soon, Petroc and Morwen were once more alone. Neither of them heard the horseman until he spoke to them.

"Petroc, son of Tobias, the King told me that I should find you here."

They span round, for one moment believing that Lord Salvis had returned.

It was not Salvis but Veritan, Lord of the Royal Palace, who slid down from the grey horse.

He was an impressive figure, a giant almost, with a gold circlet over his silver hair and piercing eyes as blue as the tunic he wore. From his belt hung his golden sword, the sword that had never yet been defeated in battle, the hilt encrusted with priceless jewels.

Petroc and Morwen stood as though turned to stone, Morwen because she had no idea who this could be and Petroc because he did know. He remembered Lord Veritan from the time he had gone to the Royal Palace with his friend, Luke. He remembered too that Lord Veritan's loyalty to the King was unshakeable and that he, Petroc, had just been saying things that were not at all loyal.

That thought prompted him to kneel, and Morwen copied him. She still did not know who it was she knelt to and she was more than a little afraid.

"Get up, both of you," Veritan said in a voice that was both kindly and stern. "You must kneel to Salvis and to the King, but not to me. I am Veritan, Lord of the King's Palace, and his messenger today."

Quickly, they scrambled to their feet. Morwen summoned up enough courage to raise her eyes to Veritan's face. To her surprise, her fear evaporated.

Petroc was not so sure. Why should the King's highest servant seek them out if it did not mean trouble?

It was as though Veritan could read his thoughts.

"Petroc, son of Tobias," he said. "The King has sent me to look for you, as you have found favour with him. He has known about the hardship you endured, first at the hand of Carrik, then by his master, Bellum. The King sees you as someone he can trust and someone deserving of reward. You remained loyal to him throughout your troubles. The King wishes to restore to you the farming land that Carrik destroyed. The King has a special purpose for your farm."

Suddenly Petroc felt very, very tired. More than anything in the world he wanted to forget the last months and put the past behind him. He could not bring himself to even think about the future.

"The King cannot bring back my father, whom Carrik killed," he said wearily. "He cannot bring back my friends whom Salvis sent away."

Veritan rubbed his chin with his hand, all the while staring keenly at Petroc. Then he looked away, over towards the Dark Forest, then again to the stronghold castle behind them. He seemed to be considering something very carefully.

"I believe there is something you must do first," he stated. "You must come with me, both of you. Come, you may ride my horse."

The horse neighed gently.

"He wants us to obey," Morwen laughed, delighted that she could sense how the horse was feeling, for she had not felt so close to the animals since Bellum had brought fear to the island by disobeying the King.

Petroc only heard a horse neighing.

Veritan helped them up, Petroc in the saddle and Morwen in front of him, holding tightly onto the horse's neck as Veritan walked beside them, leading them on. It seemed strange that the King's highest servant had given up his horse to two peasant children.

"Where are we going, lord?" Morwen ventured. She hoped it would be to the Royal Palace. She wanted so much to see Salvis again. She wanted it so much that it was like a real pain, deep inside.

"No," Veritan told her sadly. "One day, child, you will meet Salvis again, but he will never be as he was before, and it will not be today. Today we have somewhere else to go and it is in the opposite direction. I am taking you to Bellum's stronghold castle."

"No!" The words left Petroc's lips before he could stop them. "No... no lord... I cannot go back there!"

His cry disturbed the horse. It faltered briefly and then recovered beneath Veritan's restraining hand.

"Yes, you can, Petroc," Veritan said firmly and the certainty in his voice reminded them that he was here as the King's messenger and the King must be obeyed. "You will come with me to the very camp of the enemy. Bellum has no power over you any more. You have been set free. You must prove it to yourself. You must learn to trust the King."

Petroc thought *'and you have no idea what Bellum is really like. I do. I know him very well.'*

The stronghold was even darker than Petroc remembered and as he and Morwen climbed down from Veritan's horse, the boy shivered with a dreadful fear. It was only a few days since he had been set free. In that time the walls of the castle had grown higher and even more forbidding

On the other hand, Bellum, who met them at the gate of the castle, looked magnificent. Salvis' death had gone to Bellum's head – literally – for now his black hair carried a crown. It seemed strange, but the gold in the crown was dull, and the jewels did not shine. It was like a poor shadow if the King's crown.

Bellum carried a sword of black steel. His tunic was black too, and edged with gold.

Veritan and Bellum stood face to face, two giant-like figures in the kingdom of Karensa. As their eyes met it was as though lightening pierced the air. The children each gave a shiver of excitement and fear. They were fascinated yet at the same time afraid.

Quite suddenly Bellum laughed. It was unexpected and unnerving.

"So, you have come to join me, Veritan!" he roared. "Now that Salvis is dead you will need someone else to serve."

"I will never serve you, Bellum, you know that full well." Veritan's voice was as cold as the ice that forms in the Dark Forest during the Time of Snows. "Salvis is not dead. He lives and has gone to take his rightful place in the Royal Palace. Even now he sits at his father, the King's, side."

Bellum continue to laugh. "Of course he is dead!" He lifted the black sword from its scabbard. "See, my sword still carries his blood!"

Morwen felt hot tears sting her eyes at the sight of the blade of the sword which was stained dark red.

She knew in her spirit that Bellum was telling the truth and that this really was Salvis' own lifeblood that he shed when he died.

Yet as they watched, something unbelievable happened. The red stain faded and disappeared from the blade of the sword.

The children gasped. Veritan smiled triumphantly.

"See, Bellum, Salvis is no longer dead. It is as I told you. He lives again in the Royal Palace."

Bellum's eyes flickered and in his anger, their colour changed from black to amber. He knew that Veritan was telling the truth.

He glared at his sword. His face darkened. In his expression they sensed each terror of the longest night, each unspoken fear of mankind, fears past and fears to come, fears not yet created. His voice became that of the hissing serpent he had taken as his heraldic emblem.

"So the war goes on then. However, I will yet be the ruler of this island. It will be to me that the people of Karensa will turn."

Petroc and Morwen clung to each other as the air was suddenly rent by a great crash of thunder.

The thunder rumbled again and again, but it was unlike any thunder they had ever heard. This thunder was born of the fury of creation.

The ground shook violently. Wind rushed across the Meadow of Flowers, flattening wild flowers and grasses. Trees bent low as if bowing before an unseen force. The sky grew dark.

Then, with a mighty rush of wind, Bellum's crown was torn from his head and rolled away into the long grass, faster and faster through the Meadow of Flowers.

All then was quiet. The sun shone once again and the sky was blue.

"Find the crown!" Bellum roared across the still meadow, only now his voice was edged with the deep fear he had desperately been trying to hide.

Petroc and Morwen moved to obey him but Veritan pulled them back as the crown rolled away into the long grass.

"Your power is broken, Bellum," Veritan laughed. "Did you really think the King would stand by and let you take his kingdom away from him?"

"You will see my power! You will all see! You boy, Petroc, I remember you. Why have you come here? Can it be that you have come home?"

To Petroc's dismay his knees began to shake and the more he tried to stop them, the more they trembled.

His tongue clung to the roof of his mouth so that he could not speak.

Morwen replied for him. "This is not his home! This was never his home!"

Bellum sneered. "Your sister speaks in your place. Yet I recall you were not weak when you served Carrik in my stronghold. You were stubborn then, and proud. It gave us much sport to try to break your spirit, but we never did. Do you recall the night we told you how your father died? Ah, I see that you do…"

By now, Petroc was shaking visibly and hating himself for it. Morwen was staring at him, silently pleading with him to find his courage. "You did not!" he blurted at last. "You did not break me, Lord Bellum!"

"No, no we did not…" Bellum narrowed his eyes. His voice became a whisper. "Petroc, come back now. Come back with me inside the castle. I need someone like you to be at my side. Soon you will be a man. Then I will give you treasure beyond your dreams.

"See, my gates are never locked or barred. You can come and go at any time. I do not stop people coming to me as the King has done. Come back now. Not as a servant, Petroc. Not as a prisoner. Come now of your own free will. When you are a man you will walk beside me. When Karensa is really mine, you will share my glory.

"The people will bow down to me. They will worship me. They will wonder at my splendour and marvel at my music. Oh Petroc, such music… you have heard the music I can make."

He paused for breath.

"This will never be," Veritan declared resolutely.

Bellum ignored him. It was doubtful he even heard, he was so full of himself.

"What do you say, boy?" he continued. "You will not have to work. You will never have to dig and plough. And your sister too, she has a fair face. I will give her fine clothes to wear. I will teach her to make music and to dance."

His gaze made Morwen feel embarrassed. Then thankfully a picture of Salvis came into her mind and she forgot her shyness and found her courage again.

"I won't," she cried. "I won't be there! I won't ever go inside your castle!"

"Oh yes you will, Morwen." Bellum smiled lazily, still gazing at her in the same way. "One day, of your own free will, you will walk inside those gates. So will many more. The people want to live their own lives. They do not always want to be bound by the King's laws. His time is ending here."

Lord Veritan's hand reached for his sword. Then as if thinking better of it, he let it rest.

"Your power comes from mankind's fear of death and our Lord Salvis has overcome death on Karensa for ever," Veritan stated.

Bellum gave a short laugh. "Let the people choose then: pleasure now, or hardship and promises. They will choose pleasure every time. Look at this boy," he pointed a ringed finger at Petroc. "He may seem to be free but in his heart he stills belongs in my stronghold."

With those words, he turned abruptly and went back inside his castle. They heard him shout to his servants to find his fallen crown.

Morwen reached for her brother's hand and held it tight.

"You are free, Petroc. Don't believe what Bellum says," she whispered.

"He is a liar," Veritan agreed. "One day he will be known as the Father of Lies."

Petroc made a big effort to stop trembling but he was still shaking inside. He was scared. Losing his nerve was something he had never experienced before.

As Bellum's servants ran out to search for the fallen crown, Veritan helped the children back onto his horse.

They rode away, glad to see the back of this dark castle of shadows.

Veritan talked to them seriously. "The King sent me to help you, Petroc. He wants you to go back to your farm. He has issued a just decree that all lands destroyed by Bellum must be given back to the tenant farmers. You will never have to pay rent to your landlord, Carrik, again. The farm will be yours."

A flicker of interest shone in Petroc's green eyes. "Yes but, there is only me, lord, and Morwen and my mother, oh and Delfi, but she is only very small.

Farming is hard. We need a grown man to help us with the work."

Veritan laughed softly. "Oh Petroc, do not say 'yes but' to the King. The King has the answer to all things and the King will provide. Come, I will take you back through the Dark Forest."

The horse neighed softly again as they crossed the Meadow of Flowers.

More butterflies were flying towards Bellum's castle and Morwen could not resist looking back over her shoulder.

She began to wonder what the castle was really like inside.

Chapter 4

Amos

A sudden burst of bright light hurt their eyes as they left the dappled shade of the Dark Forest. In front of them was the Bay of Dolphins, or the Bay of Peace as it had been called since Salvis had lived there. It shimmered and sparkled in the hot afternoon sun.

Morwen said suddenly, "I wonder if Bellum has found his crown?"

"He will never find it, no matter how hard he searches," Veritan replied. "Now, I must return to the Royal Palace, but before I go, I believe the King has a message for each of you."

He placed his hand on Morwen's shoulders. "Child, do not let your curiosity destroy your faithfulness. Remember that loyalty to the King is the only way that leads to lasting happiness."

Next he turned to Petroc. "And you, no longer a child yet not a man, learn to trust the King. The way to overcome fear is to face it and that is what you have done by going to Bellum's castle."

"Yes, but… I was afraid," said Petroc.

"Only a fool has no fear," Veritan replied. "You did not run away, although you wanted to. You stood your ground. When you did that, Bellum could not touch you. Remember that in the days ahead."

Petroc nodded. He was feeling better about himself already.

Veritan stroked his horse and then leapt swiftly and easily onto its back.

"I am only the King's messenger. He has a task for both of you and he will provide the means to do it. The King is aware of how loyal your family has been, how faithful to his laws. Be confident that the King will help you."

He raised his hand in a gesture of farewell, turned, and in an instant he was riding like the wind through the Dark Forest.

Petroc and Morwen stared at each other. Morwen spoke first.

"Why come to us, brother? Why did such an important person come to see us?"

Petroc had no answer to give. He had been asking himself the very same question.

"Let's not go straight home," he said instead. "Let's go down to the beach. It will be cooler by the sea, sitting on the rocks."

He did not add that it was there they had last seen Salvis before he returned to the Royal Palace.

They climbed down the steep cliff path to a flat rock from where they could look out to sea.

"Petroc, why is there always a mist around the island?"

Once again she had taken him by surprise. In the old days Morwen would never have thought to ask such questions. Now they seemed to pop out without warning, like a cork from a bottle.

"Father used to say Karensa was a special place," he said thoughtfully. "He said it was a place that only a few people found, and that is why not many visitors come here."

"But I wish… I wish we could see what is on the other side of the mist. We did, just once, and there was land not too far away. If we had a boat we could sail through the mist and see what is on the other side."

"Why should we want to do that?" It had never occurred to Petroc to live anywhere but Karensa.

"I don't know. I suppose I was thinking about Rosie and Luke... Petroc, what did Bellum mean about how they told you that Father had died?"

"You are best not to know," he told her abruptly. "Anyway, I don't remember."

"Yes you do."

"I don't. Stop asking so many questions. I do not want to remember, Morwen."

Morwen said no more, but a stubborn streak made her resolve that somehow she would find out, but not today.

"Oh Petroc, don't let us be sad and argue, not today. It has been such a day! And it is wonderful that you are home again."

Again, Petroc hardened his heart.

"You go and look for shells," he said rudely. He wanted time on his own. It was one of the things his long captivity had not allowed.

Morwen sort of understood and went off quite gladly on her own.

It was not cool on the beach. If anything it was even hotter, so forgetting his pride, Petroc pulled off his boots, rolled up his trousers and paddled in the sea.

The water was wonderfully cold. The waves lapping against his bare legs were soothing. People were right to call this the Bay of Peace. It was almost as if he could still feel Salvis here, as cool and calm as the sea.

Quite unexpectedly he too began to wonder what lay beyond the mist. He had never wondered before. Karensa was his home and Karensa had always been surrounded by mist. That was how things were. He had accepted it. But now, after meeting Luke and Rosie, he was curious about other lands.

He thought for a while about his father. Tobias had been a good man. He would be pleased if they really could restore the farm.

Yet how would they? His mother was old now and could no longer work in the fields. They had a child called Delfi staying with them who his mother had taken under her wing, but Delfi was too small to work. He and Morwen could not do all the work on their own.

Besides which, he was not at all sure he wanted Salvis or the King to help him. In Bellum's castle they had heard about Salvis and the army he was gathering in the Bay of Dolphins which they now called the Bay of Peace. They had dreams that one day Salvis' army would fight Bellum and set them free.

Sadly, things had not gone that way. It was Salvis who had died and as soon as he was captured, his brave army had run away.

Morwen lay on her stomach and leant over a rock pool. In the still water she could see her reflection as clear as in a mirror. She studied herself with a critical eye. She saw an oval face sprinkled with freckles and surrounded by a coronet of red-gold hair. She saw light green eyes, a small neat nose and a mouth that was both full and wide. She was surprised and pleased to realise that Bellum had been right. She was pretty.

Again, as at the castle, a picture of Salvis came into her mind. She jumped up.

"Petroc, I'm going home. Mother will need me to help cook our meal."

Martha did not need her daughter's help after all because the meal was ready. All that was needed on such a hot day was cheese, crusty brown bread and fruit, all of which were plentiful

Petroc ran and caught up with her and together they peered into the sudden darkness of the cave house. The boy was still weak. The hard climb up the cliff steps had left him breathless.

Thankfully, he sat down at the wooden table, trying to hide how out of breath he really was. It was only then that both he and Morwen realised that a visitor sat in the shadows at the back of the cave.

"Uncle Amos!" Morwen threw herself at him, suddenly a child again. "What brings you here?"

The big, red-headed, red-bearded man laughed loudly. Everything Amos did was loud.

"Maiden, you grow too old for such wild behaviour!" he exclaimed. "Why, you have taken the air clean out of my chest! Stand back now so I may look at you, for I think you have grown tall. Soon you will be a young woman and then some young man shall come and steal you away!"

Morwen blushed. "Uncle, I am only twelve!" she protested, but not before she thought about Luke. She had thought that when they grew up they might be more than friends, but it seemed that this was not to be.

Amos turned his attention to Petroc and the laughter died on his lips.

He sighed. "Oh, what has happened to you, boy?"

"You know what happened, Uncle!" Petroc twisted his mouth into a wry smile.

"Was Carrik so harsh to you?"

Petroc was beginning to feel embarrassed. "Bellum was harsh," he muttered tersely. "Look, I have left something on the beach. I'll fetch it. Don't wait for me. You start your meal."

He almost ran from the house, setting aside his tiredness in his panic to get away, and ignoring Martha's call to him to return.

Amos put his hand on Morwen's arm.

"We should leave him. I was thoughtless in what I said, but it was the shock of seeing him so… so thin and pale. In a moment I shall seek him out and put things right. No, better still, I shall go now."

He hurried after Petroc. Martha and Morwen heard his voice bellowing across the beach and exchanged worried looks for they both thought that Petroc needed time on his own.

Not for the first time Morwen thought that her mother looked very tired. Her hair, once red, was now almost grey. The brown tunic and trousers she wore hung loosely from her shoulders, for once she had been plump and now she was thin.

She hesitated. "Mother, you are not ill, are you?"

Martha shrugged. "I do not know, child. At times it seems that all my energy is spent. Still," she gestured to the dark haired child who rarely left her side. "I have Delfi here. She is a great comfort to me."

"I try to be," the little girl said shyly. "You took me in when no-one else would have me… after my father left…"

Neither Martha nor Morwen were cruel enough to say that Delfi's father, Josh, had not simply left. He had betrayed Salvis and run away and had not been see since.

"There, my lamb, it was not your doing," Martha said softly.

Morwen sat down on the chair that her brother had just vacated.

"Mother, why is Uncle Amos here?"

"He has an idea to put to us. He has come all the way from his home on the far side of the island with great plans, but he shall tell you of them when he returns. It may mean we have to leave here."

Morwen looked around. It was a poor enough place, but the house built in a cave had been their home for more than half a year. It was basic; only a front and back built on the cave. They had slept on straw, dry seaweed and furs and no matter how often they washed, they always seemed to smell of fish.

But it was safe. No-one could attack them here. Not Bellum, not Carrik, not anyone. It had been their safe house after Tobias had died.

"Mother, Delfi, you would never believe what happened today," she said. She told them all about Veritan and Bellum and all the things that had been said.

Martha listened intently, sometimes nodding, sometimes exclaiming her disbelief.

"You should keep away from that Lord Bellum and his ideas," was her only comment. "No good shall ever come of talking to that one. As for the rest of it, I think you will be surprised when you hear what your Uncle Amos has to say."

"Delfi tugged Martha's sleeve. "I think... I think Petroc misses Luke and Rosie."

"Yes he does," Martha replied. "I am going to tell you two a secret, but you must promise not to tell a soul."

"We promise," they chorused eagerly.

"Well, I once went to see the King."

"Mother, when? You never said!"

"No, well it was a secret. It was before our last Time of Gathering. I went for Petroc."

"Why?"

"Now this is a secret, mind? I had the notion that maybe Petroc was lonely, that he needed a friend. He was always so busy helping his father that he had no time to make friends. So, I went to the King and asked for a friend for my son. Then, a little while later, Luke and Rosie came to stay."

"That must be why the King sent them to live in our house!" gasped Morwen.

"I think partly that, partly for other reasons. But it did mean that Petroc found a friend."

Delfi nodded. "That is why Petroc misses them so much now they have gone home."

"I suppose it could be. But we have to remember that it is all part of the King's great plan for everyone... Listen, Uncle Amos and Petroc are coming back now. A secret, remember? Not a word. You must never give a secret away when someone has trusted it to you."

A dark head and a red head nodded in unison, but the girls could not resist exchanging meaningful nudges when the boy walked through the door.

Petroc hardly noticed them as he sat down near Morwen, for he seemed to have found a new energy. His eyes were bright with excitement.

"Mother, Uncle Amos has told me why he is here. He has come to help us restore our farm!"

Morwen's heart thumped so loudly that she was surprised the others did not hear it. She could almost see her heart beating through her tunic.

She gave a little cry. Only this day, Veritan had promised that the King would help them and neither of them had really believed him.

Now help was here.

Chapter 5

Memories and Plans

The early morning air smelled of new life, of gulls and fish and seaweed and of the mist that hung low over the bay, but Petroc and Morwen had no time to linger on the beach. They had a long way to go and strode off purposefully in the direction of their farm, which was many hours' walk away.

Last night there had been a long discussion about whether or not they should be allowed to go on their own.

Amos thought that he should go with them, but Martha had finally convinced him that this was something the children needed to do alone.

Neither of them had been home since Tobias had died. If nothing else, they needed to see where he was sleeping.

They chose the coastal path. Sometimes the sea was in view and at other times it was hidden behind houses or trees. As the sun grew high in the sky the mist rolled back to the horizon and once more the air was warm

For the most part they walked in silence, each lost in their own memories. It was only when they stopped on a grassy cliff to eat their food that Morwen dared voice her thoughts.

"It all seems so long ago; Father, the farm, our visitors… we have not been home for so long. Will it still look the same?"

"I don't know. It cannot be the same if Bellum set fire to it as you said."

"So what do we do then?"

"We build it again," Petroc replied resolutely. "Our father's grandfather built that farm from nothing. That is what we shall do. What our great grandfather could do, we can do also."

"Yes, but times were different then. Karensa was still loyal to the King. He still dealt with people's problems each night at the Time of Decisions. The ground was rich. Now, I hear tell there are many stones and thistles which choke the corn."

"Stones can be removed. Thistles can be pulled up. Rebuild the farm. That is what we have to do."

Morwen considered this. "Lord Veritan did say it was what the King wanted us do."

"Not for the King! Not for Veritan. Not for Salvis, either," her brother replied. "We shall do this for Father."

"What did Uncle Amos say to you, Petroc?"

Petroc stared out to sea. "He said that he is here for Mother. The war did not really touch the far side of the island where he lives, but of course he knew that Father was gone and the farm destroyed. Now that the war is over and all the lost lands restored to the tenants, well then, Uncle Amos knew that getting our farm started again was the right thing to do. Our cousins are old enough to take care of Amos' own farm while he is away. That's it, really."

"Maybe the King – "

"Oh, the King, the King!" Petroc was getting annoyed again. "Listen Morwen, Uncle Amos said other things too. He said that on the far side of the island they live to help each other and do not think too much about Salvis or Bellum or the King. They help each other in need." He lowered his voice to almost a whisper. "Morwen, all I know is that our father, Tobias, was a good, kind man. He took care of us and provided for us and… and he loved us. He would want us to start up the farm again. So we do this for him."

When she said nothing, he went on, "Morwen, forget all about Salvis and I shall forget Bellum and Carrik and all the bad things that happened to me."

Morwen still did not speak.

"We shall both make a new start," Petroc insisted. "This last year has changed both of us. We've had to stop being children and grow up. I know I've changed–"

"Yes you have! You were never so hard of heart!"

"You have changed too. Once you were shy and obedient. Now you are bold."

She was surprised. "Am I?"

"Yes, sister, you are. Look at the way you spoke up to Bellum. You would never have done that a year ago. And yes, you are right; I have become hard. We must face life as it really is. We have enough food and money put by to last us through until this time next year but then we shall have to reap our own harvest. Mother grows frail. Think of the years she worked with Father out in the fields, or got up before dawn to milk the cows. We owe it to her and Father to rebuild the farm."

Morwen could not argue with that.

"Come then, brother, pack away the rest of the meal. As always, Mother has given plenty. Do you want a last drink of water before I put it away?"

"No save it. Let's not waste any more time. Morwen, let's go home."

But when they arrived home, things were much, much worse than they had imagined.

All that remained of the farmhouse was a stone shell, blackened by fire, over which ivy crept at random. The roof had gone completely. The only part left intact was the outside barn

In stunned silence they approached the place where the door used to be. There, to the left of the building, was a grassy mound of earth. At one end someone had placed two sticks tied together to form a cross. They knew without doubt that this was their father's grave.

Petroc bent down to touch the wooden cross.

"What is this… this… this thing here for?"

"No, leave it!" Morwen said quickly. "See, it has been tied with a red ribbon. That was Rosie's hair ribbon. She must have put it here for a purpose."

"But what does it mean?"

"I don't know. I think it may have something to do with Salvis. Oh leave it, Petroc, please!"

He shrugged. He was not really bothered either way.

For quite a long time they stood close together just looking at the grave, each with their own memories of their father and the life they had once loved. Neither of them cried. Morwen had shed all her tears when Tobias had died. Petroc had no tears to shed.

Eventually he put his thin arm around her shoulders.

"Father is not here, Morwen. He's gone. It is only his shell that remains in there."

"I know," she whispered, "but I wanted to say goodbye. He was harsh sometimes, but he was a good father to us and I loved him very much. He did nothing that was not for our good. I know that now."

"So do I, and that is why we shall do his work, not because the King told us to, or Veritan, or Salvis."

Morwen did not agree. To her the most important thing was to obey Salvis, but she thought it wise not to say so.

A sudden noise behind them made them jump. Too late they saw the remains of their dinner disappearing in the arms of a scrawny boy.

They raced after him. He was small, so it did not take Petroc long to catch him. In no time at all he tackled the thief and had him on the ground.

The boy lay very still. Morwen stared accusingly at Petroc.

"I didn't hurt him," Petroc protested. "Truly, Morwen, I did him no harm."

The boy's face was very white. He was thin and had a mop of curly black hair.

Morwen knelt down by his side. "Oh Petroc, it's not a boy. It's a girl. I think she has fainted. I wonder when she last had food?"

Petroc stared. He realised it was only the girl's short hair that made him think she was a boy.

"Wait a minute – I know this girl! She… she was in Bellum's castle with me. She was a prisoner, just like me. Her name is Cherry. She served a woman called Nolis. That's who cut off her hair."

"Why?" Morwen asked.

"Oh, it was the woman's brother, Tas. He admired Cherry's hair so Nolis cut it off. I do remember her."

Cherry moaned softly.

"Quickly, get the water," Morwen commanded.

As Cherry struggled to sit up, Petroc cradled her on his lap and helped her to drink from the flask. There was a new tenderness about him. It was as though at last he had found someone who understood him.

The girl had very large, dark eyes and she stared weakly at Morwen.

"Are you hungry?" Morwen asked. "When did you last have a meal?"

Cherry shook her head as if she was trying to remember and could not.

Morwen gave her the remainder of the bread and cheese and she devoured them greedily. Now that the rosy colour was returning to her lips and cheeks, they could see why she was called Cherry.

She twisted round to see who it was that held her.

"Petroc? You here?" she gasped.

"This is my farm, Cherry," he said sternly, but in a way that made it clear that he meant her no harm. "You are on my land. And you tried to steal our food. That does not matter because we understand you were very hungry, but what are you doing on my farm?"

Morwen noted that he now said 'my' farm not 'our' farm.

Cherry sank back against him. "I had nowhere to go. When we were set free –when Salvis died- I left with the others, but I had no home to go to. I walked and walked then I found this place. I have been living here, sleeping over there." She pointed to the barn. "Does it really matter, Petroc? After all we suffered in Bellum's castle, after all the things we saw them do, after all the times we were treated roughly and left hungry, does it really matter that I slept in your barn? Or that I ate your dinner and stole apples from your trees? Oh yes, there are apples there. Does it matter though, Petroc? Surely what really matters is that we are free?"

He put her gently to one side and rose to his feet. He did not want to be reminded of things that had happened in Bellum's castle. Furthermore, he did not want his sister to know about them either.

"I need time to think," he said thickly. "Both of you wait for me here."

He strode away from the farm as fast as his thin legs would go.

Chapter 6

Cherry's Story

Cherry and Morwen stared at each other in dismay. They had both jumped to their feet when Petroc had walked away.

"We should follow him," Morwen said uncertainly.

"No, he's better alone. We should leave him."

Morwen was irritated that this girl should think that she knew Petroc better than his own sister with whom he had grown up.

Cherry must have guessed her thoughts. "I know how he feels," she explained. "I feel it too sometimes; sort of panicky, like I just have to run away."

"He never used to be like that," said Morwen.

"Things are not as they used to be. I was different too, before... before..."

Suddenly, Morwen was curious. "Let's sit down under the trees," she suggested. "You can tell me your story and I'll tell you about me. I thought you were a boy!"

"That's my hair," Cherry replied ruefully. "Nolis cut it all off. It was shorter than this once. At least now it has started to grow again."

"Who is Nolis?"

Cherry led the way to what had once been the orchard.

"You're limping!" Morwen cried.

"Yes. It was always so. It never bothered me before but somehow, when we went to live with Bellum, it got much worse. I can run well enough. It is when I walk slowly that it shows up the most."

They sat down in the shade, with their backs to a large apple tree. The air was sweet with the smell of ripe fruit and warm sun and the hum of bees.

"Tell me who Nolis is," Morwen prompted.

"Very well, I'll tell you about me and then it is your turn...

"My father was chief steward in a big household on the far side of the island. When I was little my life was so happy! Our master and mistress were good, kind people. They had a daughter called Zena who often looked after me when I was small. We wanted for nothing."

Cherry's lips trembled, but she struggled on with her story.

"When Zena grew up she married Tas, a woodcutter. She believed herself to be in love with him, I suppose, and she would not listen to her parents when they told her she was wrong. They were not the sort of people to forbid her anything that she had set her heart on, so she went ahead with their blessing. I was given to Zena as her personal maidservant and went to live with her and her husband, Tas."

Cherry faltered again but Morwen waited patiently for her to recover.

"Tas was horrible, right from the start. He had a sister called Nolis and she hated Zena, probably because Zena is pretty and Nolis is plain. Nolis made her life and mine as hard as she could, and Tas always took her part against poor Zena.

Once, Zena made herself a beautiful cloak. She spent hours sewing it. When it was finished Nolis tried to claim it for her own. It is the only time I ever saw Zena get angry. She was really upset. Tas took them both to the King at the Time of Decisions and it was on that night that Lord Bellum started the war. We never returned to the woodcutter's cottage. We went directly with Bellum. Tas helped him chop down trees for wood to build the fortifications around his castle."

Again she paused.

"Take your time. It is a long story," Morwen said to encourage her.

Cherry nodded and took a deep breath. "In Bellum's castle it was even worse. Tas took me away from Zena and made me work for Nolis. I was never allowed to speak to Zena again." Her voice grew very faint and she brushed away the tears that were spilling from her huge, dark eyes.

Morwen gave her hand a gentle squeeze. All at once her problems did not seem so important. But there was one thing she was burning to ask.

"Cherry, the night they told Petroc that Father had died, what did happen?"

Cherry sighed sadly. "Oh, that was the night Carrik moved to Bellum's castle. He brought Petroc with him. There must have been some sort of trouble on the way there, I do not know, something to do with some visitors from the world beyond the mist."

"Luke and Rosie?"

"That's right. I am not sure exactly what happened. They brought another prisoner but we never saw him. He was locked away in a cell deep beneath the castle. Later they said Bellum had him put to death."

"Kett? It must have been Kett!" The cave house where they were living once belonged to a man called Kett who had helped them.

"I do not know," Cherry admitted. "But that night there was a feast in the Great Hall. There was singing and dancing – ah yes," now her voice was bitter, "Bellum can make music sweet enough to charm a mountain of stone.

"But that night they were angry with Petroc. Carrik was especially angry with him. He took him to the platform at the front of the hall, where everyone could see him, and stood him there on his own. Then he called for silence. When it was fully quiet he told Petroc that his father had died and that he, Carrik, was the one who had killed him.

There was nothing Petroc could do because Carrik was guarded by men with swords. Everyone laughed, because they had all drunk too much wine and then some of them began to throw food at him and he just stood there. It was terrible. He had to stand there for hours before they would let him step down…

But Morwen, he did not cry. His face was very white but he never let them see him cry. Only later, in the big room where they locked up the youngest captives for the night, then I heard him weeping in the dark."

Morwen covered her face with her hands. She was sobbing, because her heart was breaking for her brother and yet at the same time she was so proud of him.

"Not once," Cherry whispered. "Not once did he betray Salvis or the King."

"There is still time for betrayal."

The girls leapt to their feet. Neither had been aware of horsemen approaching.

Through her tears, Morwen recognised the speaker and her heart sank into her boots.

"It's Carrik! What's he doing here?" she hissed under her breath.

The thin, middle-aged man overheard and looked mildly surprised. He spoke to his companion, a youth on a grey pony, and they both laughed.

"My dear child," he said to Morwen. "Why should I not be here? This is after all my land."

Morwen found courage from somewhere. "It is not your land! The King has given all captured lands to the rightful tenants. That means it is now our land!"

Morwen was actually very afraid but tried not to show it. The last time she had met Carrik he had stolen grain from the farm and then carried her brother off as his prisoner. But today there seemed to be nothing so fearsome about him. Maybe he had changed?

Carrik shrugged carelessly. "What does that matter? I have wealth to spare. Bellum is a generous master. You are welcome to such a meagre farm, you and your brother. I doubt you will ever make a living from it though. Where is your brother, Petroc, by the way?"

"I do not know and if I did, I should not tell you. Neither would Cherry."

Carrik laughed again. "Dear child, do not be so disturbed by my question. I am really not concerned. Come, Esram, we have other work to do."

The horse and pony turned and trotted off in the direction of High Hill.

The two girls sank to the ground. Their knees seemed to give way beneath them. They were both trembling.

"I hate that man!" Cherry cried.

"He does not seem as bad as I thought…"

"Oh Morwen, do not be deceived. He has not changed. And that boy, I hate him even more!"

"Who is he?"

"His name is Esram. He is Carrik's nephew. He tormented all of us children while we were prisoners and could do nothing in return. He is worse than

Carrik. He hates the King and he hates Salvis and all those who serve him."

"He carried a net on his pony. What is that for?"

"You may well ask! It was his favourite pastime. He would hide and wait until one of us came along carrying food or wine then he would catch us in his net. Whatever we were carrying would be spoilt. We would be punished for spoiling it and Esram would stand and laugh."

"He sounds awful! Cherry, they have gone towards High Hill and I don't know for sure, but that may be where Petroc has gone."

Chapter 7

Esram

Petroc had not expected High Hill to be covered with thistles. There had been no thistles when he had sat here with Luke, the night the war had started. Now thistles and stones and weeds were everywhere, and this would make farming much harder than it was before.

He found a clear, grassy spot and sat down with his back resting against the steep slope of the hill. Just as Petroc wanted to forget the last months, he seemed to be reminded of them more and more.

Cherry was the last person he had wanted to see.

Even so, he knew they had to take care of her. They could not leave her to fend for herself, for she was almost starving, and he had already decided that tonight she must go back to the cave house. His mother would make her welcome there. She would have enough to eat and somewhere dry to sleep.

Sitting here, he could not help but think about Luke. Where was he now? Somewhere, on the other side of the mist that surrounded Karensa, was a whole world that they knew very little about. Luke had told him strange stories of things called computers, and supper cooked in a microwave oven - whatever that was - and fast food, and televisions; of places they called schools where all the children were made to go every day; of things called cars that you sat in and they took you

47

from place to place so you did not have to walk; of webcams and Bluetooth –why would anyone want blue teeth? Oh, and reality shows, Luke had talked a lot about reality shows.

Sometimes Petroc felt as though he was in a reality show now. Part of him seemed to be here, part of him seemed to be back at the farm with his father and part of him seemed to be with Bellum and Carrik. It was difficult to tell just what was real.

A pale pink butterfly settled on his arm and then flew away. Petroc watched it dancing from leaf to leaf. Bees were busy taking pollen from the wild flowers and the faint hum of insects made him feel drowsy. He put his hands behind his head and closed his eyes so that the bright sun shone red behind his eyelids. Sleep was good. Sleep made him forget the past.

He awoke with a shock as the heavy net fell over his face. As he struggled, he felt the net being pulled tight around him so that he could not move his arms. Fear and panic rushed through him, numbing his senses. In his mind he was back in Bellum's stronghold. It was no use struggling. The net was too strong and, taken by surprise as he was, he could not escape.

"Hah! Petroc! I have you at last!"

It was the voice he hated more than any other, Esram, Carrik's nephew. He was only a year older than Petroc, yet he had caused more trouble than all Carrik's household together. This net had been his favourite sport.

Petroc glared fiercely from beneath its heavy folds and sure enough the thin faced, fair haired figure of Esram was grinning down at him.

From a place deep inside, Petroc instinctively did what he had done so many times before when he had felt like giving up. Silently he called to the one person he knew would help him. Without words and in his heart he cried out to the King.

At once new energy flowed through him, and with strength more than his own strength and power more than his own power, he pulled off the net and broke free.

He threw himself at Esram before the older boy had time to gather his thoughts. Over and over they tumbled, their faces and arms scratched by thorns and thistles and stung by nettles. Neither would give in as they rolled down the steep slope of High Hill, locked together in combat. By the time they landed at the bottom, Esram's nose was streaming with blood and Petroc had a black eye. Still they continued to fight, punching and kicking until at last Carrik stepped forward to pull Esram away and Cherry and Morwen arrived and dragged off Petroc.

The two boys rested for a minute, then Petroc sprang at Esram again, all his pent-up feelings now released, and in spite of all efforts to stop them they were once more grappling on the ground,

Morwen, watching helplessly, gasped in horror as she saw her brother take a fishing knife from his belt and hold it to the other boy's throat.

Esram's face was white with fear but before anyone could make a move to stop the fight, they heard another voice.

"Enough! In the name of the King, stop this!"

Both boys froze with horror. Lord Veritan stood in front of them, his own face pale with anger and his golden sword drawn ready for battle.

"This is not the way!" he cried. "Nothing is gained by creating war. Petroc put that knife away and see that you keep it for the purpose for which it was made. And get up, both of you!"

Carrik obviously had no intention of being overshadowed by a mere Lord of the Palace. He cleared his throat.

"I told you to stop fighting," he said, lying to regain Veritan's respect. Without Veritan he would have been as much use as a flea in a bowl of broth, as Martha would say.

Lord Veritan ignored him. Esram and Petroc stood up and glared at each other. Both of them had torn clothes and both were bruised and bloodstained.

Petroc did as Veritan told him and put his fishing knife back in his belt.

"You, Esram," Veritan pointed to the fair haired youth. "Give that net to your uncle and do not ever use it again. You have caused mischief enough with it. Carrik, take this boy back where he belongs."

Esram opened his mouth as if he wanted to argue but then he seemed to change his mind. His uncle led the horse and the pony forward and they mounted up.

Before turning away, Carrik saluted Veritan.

"You serve one master, Veritan, I serve another," he said softly, almost pleasantly. "We shall see which master wins the war."

"The outcome is already decided, Carrik," Veritan replied. "All that is left is to declare our allegiance. Who is for Bellum; who is for the King?"

Carrik inclined his head. "Many will be for Bellum," he replied, but without malice, then he and Esram left quickly.

"As for you Petroc," said Veritan, "you know what you have to do. Begin the work the King has given you and he will provide all the tools you need."

Before the children had time to ask any more questions, he too was gone.

"Well," said Cherry, "just who was that?"

She was standing with her hands on her hips and her head to one side. She looked so funny with her short, cropped hair and red cheeks that both Petroc and Morwen burst out laughing.

Then Petroc groaned for Esram had landed several hard kicks to his ribs and it hurt to laugh.

"We should go back to the farm," he murmured. "I need to sit down."

He limped back like a wounded soldier with Morwen holding him on one side and Cherry on the other.

Thankfully, he sat down in the barn. Morwen washed his scratched face and arms while Cherry took the wide linen belt from her tunic and bound his ribs.

Their old well had remained fresh and clean and they filled the flask and gave it to him to drink.

"Is this where you have been living, Cherry?" Morwen asked.

She nodded. "It is dry and warm. Lonely though, especially at night, when… when the…"

"When the bad dreams come," Petroc finished for her.

She nodded again.

"I have them too," he told her. It was the first time he had admitted this to anyone. "Cherry, you won't ever be alone again. I have made up my mind. This farm is my home. Now that my father, Tobias, is dead, I am the rightful farmer and I will not leave it again. Tonight I shall sleep here in the barn. You will go back to the Bay of Dolphins with Morwen and fetch Mother and Delfi and Uncle Amos. Then tomorrow, we shall start to rebuild our home."

Chapter 8

New Power

Petroc shivered and pulled the rough woollen blanket tightly around his thin shoulders. He had spent an uncomfortable night alone in the barn, drifting in and out of sleep, and each sleep troubled by dreams; first of Tobias, then of Salvis, then of Carrik and Bellum and Luke.

And Esram; always there was Esram, threading his way through each dream like a snake, so much like Luke in his appearance but a million miles apart in any other way.

Petroc's ribs still hurt where Esram had kicked him yesterday and, to make things even worse, the night had turned unexpectedly cold. Once he was awake, it had been difficult to get back to sleep. Now he was tired.

As he unwillingly forced himself to wake up, he realised that it must be quite late. The sun was already streaming through the high open window of the barn. He yawned and sat up, wincing with pain from his many bruises. It was still chilly and he wrapped the blanket around himself like a cloak.

He was very hungry. The girls had left the water flask with him and he drank deeply, then he picked two large apples from the tree, and the water and the apples were his breakfast; all the food he had. They did not satisfy his hunger but they would have to do.

He began to understand how Cherry must have felt with only fruit and water for food. Even in Bellum's castle they were able to eat the leftover scraps.

He splashed cold water from the well on his face to help him wake up and to bathe his eye, which was sore.

The girls had not been happy to leave him here, especially Cherry, who had been sent away to a strange home with someone she had only just met, but Petroc was adamant. Something had happened to him when he called to the King, it was almost as though his old fighting spirit had returned.

He decided to inspect the farmhouse and he paused at Tobias' grave.

"Oh, Father, I know this is what you would want," he whispered. "I know this will bring peace to your spirit, just as it does to me."

The damage to the farmhouse was as bad as it could possibly be. The first thing they must do was replace the roof and front door, then make shutters for the windows. Where would they start? What would they use? They would need wood and thatch and ropes and ladders, not to mention hammers and saws.

There was no longer an upstairs, for its floor had been completely destroyed by the fire. The bedroom where he had slept with its window looking out to the stars, that was gone forever.

A sudden noise sent him to the doorway. Clattering across the yard was the oldest, most battered cart he had ever seen. On it, in the middle of a huge pile of belongings, sat Martha and Delfi. The cart was being pulled by Amos who had harnessed himself to the shaft, and it was being pushed by Cherry and Morwen. They must have left the Bay of Dolphins before dawn.

Cherry waved. "Petroc, it's us! We're here!"

"I can see that," he grinned, and ran to meet them. "Here, let me take the back of the cart."

"We have pushed it all the way from the Bay of Dolphins so we can push it across the yard," Cherry replied crossly. "Besides, your ribs must hurt."

She was right. Each breath Petroc took seemed to bring with it more pain.

"Where did you get it? We don't have a cart any more."

Delfi replied. "It belonged to my father, Josh," she whispered. "He will not need it, so we borrowed it."

There was an awkward silence at the mention of Josh, the traitor's name. Josh had disappeared when Salvis died and no-one had seen him since, though many rumours were being spread around.

Morwen helped first Martha and then Delfi down from the cart and it was suddenly brought home to Petroc how old and frail his mother had become. When had she become so old? Was it when he had been captured by Carrik or was it when Tobias was killed?

"Mother, you should sit down," he said, and went to help her but she pushed him away.

"Boy, it would seem that you are the one needing help. Look at you! You can hardly walk. Who blackened your eye?"

"It is a long story," Petroc said ruefully, "and the one who did this came off worse... I think."

Martha had forgotten him. She was staring at what remained of their home.

"Oh, Petroc, what shall we do? We have no house left! Carrik has taken it all!"

Amos stepped up to speak. He had been finding his breath again after the long, gruelling walk. The cart had been heavy and he was no longer a young man.

Folk seemed to grow old so quickly in these troubled times.

"Things are not so bad, sister," he said with a confidence that he did not feel. "The first thing we must do it to get a roof on, the rest may follow later."

"But how will it, Amos?" Martha cried, very close to tears. "Oh Amos, Amos, it is hopeless!"

Morwen alone was undismayed. "Lord Veritan said that we should begin work and the King would send all the help we would need. That is what we should do."

Her brother laughed mockingly. "Oh yes? And will Veritan chop the wood? And cut the reeds for thatch?"

"No," Morwen said quietly, "but it seems there are those who will." She pointed across the field towards the Dark Forest. "See, there are people coming even now from the farms."

They arrived silently, a long line of those who had once been their neighbours and friends. Some carried timber, some rushes, flax and straw, some tools, others grain and food. Some even had money to give.

There was Raldi the carpenter; Martha had fed his children when he had no work. There was Simeon the boatman; Tobias had rescued his pet dog when it had fallen through thin ice into the river during the Time of Snows. And Mara; Morwen had befriended her daughter when she was slow learning to walk. And Daris, from the farm next to theirs; Petroc had helped mend his fences after a storm.

Raldi was their leader and spoke for them all.

"We heard you had returned. Tobias was a good man and loyal to the King as are we. We have come to repay your kindness to us. By tonight your house shall have its roof. Come friends, we shall set to work."

Morwen's heart sang. "The King did not desert us!" she exclaimed joyfully.

****

Far away in the Royal Palace the King spoke to Salvis and to the Unseen Lord of the Third Throne.

"It is time. Now my people are ready to receive my Power."

"It is time," Salvis agreed.

The assembled servants dropped to their knees and bowed their heads to the ground as the King and Salvis each raised their right hands, palms outward, towards the Unseen Lord of the Third Throne.

This Unseen Lord moved, and the Hall's silver light deepened to the colour of fire, and flames were sent from the thrones so that the marble floor turned red as blood. A mighty rush of wind travelled three times around the Hall.

Then it was still and quiet. The King and Salvis joined their hands and held them across the Third Throne. The Three were still One and the One was still Three and yet power had been sent out from the Third Throne: a power that would be given to the people of Karensa to fight against the enemy and a power that could change each of their lives.

****

Petroc and Morwen stood with their backs resting against the new front door.

Morwen shook her head almost in disbelief.

"Brother it seems the impossible has come about. We have a roof, we have a door and we have shutters on the windows. We even have a table and benches made from the leftover wood. Oh, the King has been so good to us!"

Petroc had never expected them to accomplish so much in a day, but he was grateful to their friends.

"It was not the King! It was people returning our kindness," he snapped. "It is them we should thank, Morwen, not the King."

"The King… The King…" Morwen struggled for the right words. "The King organised it," she said at last, and went to help Martha with the supper before he could shout her down.

They had brought plates, beakers and cooking pots from the cave house and Martha had cooked a fine supper of meat and vegetables, crusty bread and sweet fruit pies she had baked last night before going to bed.

All of their friends were invited to stay. They sat around the long table and as it grew dark, Martha lit the candles she had brought.

Petroc honoured Amos by giving him the place at the head of the table which should have been his own seat as the only son of Tobias and head of the family.

Just as they were about to eat, Amos stood up.

"My friends, we thank you for your help," he said simply. "Martha's family now has a home, the home that belongs to them by right. Without your help we could not have done this work. Eat now. Eat your fill of what we have all provided."

"One moment, brother," Martha pulled at his sleeve. "Before we begin, should we not remember Salvis? He was so good to us. He gave us hope when there was none. He healed us when we were sick. He encouraged us. Now he has given my family back their home."

"You are right," Raldi agreed. "When we all ran away he went to meet Bellum on his own."

"We must never forget him," Martha added.

Cherry said, "I saw him die. To the end he cared for each one of us."

Petroc felt anger rising in the very pit of his stomach. He too had waited on Salvis to deliver them, all those months in Bellum's stronghold he had waited and trusted in Salvis, but Salvis had not fought to take back that which was his own.

Not wishing to upset Martha, Petroc slipped out quietly and went for a walk. When he had calmed down he remembered that he was still hungry and that he needed his supper, so he went back to the farm, hoping to slip in without being noticed.

At once he knew that something had happened. Inside the farmhouse there was an air of excitement and laughter. There was a special atmosphere that he had never experienced before. It was like stepping into a warm bath.

"Oh Petroc," Morwen cried. "Petroc, Salvis has been here! We did not see him but he has given is his power!"

"It was like a fire," Cherry exclaimed. "His power came to each of us like a fire!"

Raldi and his friends seemed to have gone completely mad. They were dancing and singing in strange new words that Petroc had never heard before, as though they had drunk too much wine. Yet there had been no wine with the meal.

Even Martha was changed. The years seemed to have melted away and once more she was the mother Petroc remembered.

"My son, it is true! The King has given us his own power. It is here, in our hearts!"

She threw her arms around him so that he cried out in pain for his ribs were still very sore. Then she did an amazing thing. She put her hands on the very place where it hurt and a sensation like pins and needles travelled through his body.

"Salvis would not want you to be hurt," she said.

He pulled away.

"You are imagining things, all of you! Salvis is not here. You just wish he was, that is all. Salvis is dead."

"Oh Petroc," said Morwen sadly, "you know he is alive. You saw him yourself on the beach."

"It was a ghost," he argued. "Look, when I can touch him, when I see him eating and drinking with us, then I shall believe he is alive. Not until then."

The strange thing was that his ribs no longer hurt.

Chapter 9

Ploughing and Planting

The days became weeks and the weeks became months and soon the Time of Plenty became the Time of Gathering. Now the hedgerows on the island of Karensa were bright with berries and the mornings were misty and cool.

Now the farm looked more like the home where Petroc and Morwen had grown up. Although the house was still without a first floor, Morwen and Cherry had made partitions from old blankets which Martha had brought back with her from the cave house. Amos and Petroc had a bedroom in one far corner of the large room and Martha and the girls slept in another corner.

Martha made rugs for the floor to keep them warm when the Time of Snows arrived. Amos rebuilt the tiny wash-house and there was always a fire with hot water to wash themselves and their clothes.

In the fields, Amos and Petroc, Morwen and Cherry worked hard from dawn to dusk. Fences were repaired and walls rebuilt with dry stones. With two old ploughs given to them by Raldi the carpenter, the four of them managed to plough two of the three fields they owned. They would leave the third field fallow until next year.

It was back breaking work. They had no horses or oxen, so the ploughs had to be pulled by hand, each taking turns to be harnessed. By the time both fields were done, the girls especially felt there was not a muscle or bone in their bodies that did not hurt.

Still, it was done! It was at last done!

Petroc had grown strong again. The hard work had built up his muscles and Martha's cooking had filled him out so that he was no longer weak and spindly.

Cherry suffered the most. Her foot now seemed even lamer, but she never complained, even though the others could tell that it hurt.

With the money their friends had given them on the day the roof was built, they bought chickens for the yard so they had a supply of fresh brown eggs. They also bought a few sheep that would give them fine lambs before the Time of New Birth next year. They had a goat, so there was milk every day. They had enough money to buy seed and then still some left over.

Each evening at supper time, they would speak of all the good things that the King and Salvis had brought into their lives, for they were sure that this was all due to the King's blessing. Had he not set Lord Veritan to tell them what to do? He had promised them they would have all they needed and they did, and still more.

One day in every seven, the friends who had helped them would come to the farmhouse with their families, and they would talk about the King and of Salvis, his son. Sometimes Delfi would sing while Cherry played a lyre. Cherry was very musical. She would even make up songs for Delfi to sing, songs about Salvis.

More and more people joined them until the farmhouse was full to overflowing with praises to the King.

People were changed. They seemed to have found new strength within. They had no fear of each other, just as there had been no fear on the island before the war.

As new people joined, they too received the King's Power. Sometimes they would sing in a wonderful new language they had been given; a special language with words of ancient days. Singing in this way seemed to give them even more power and energy.

Petroc alone did not change. He still waited to see Salvis with his own eyes and touch him with his own hands before he believed.

One day they went to gather blackberries, Petroc and Morwen, Cherry and Delfi. They walked to the cliffs overlooking Black Rock Bay, where brambles were heavy with fruit. They had filled their baskets and their mouths were stained purple from berries they had eaten.

Cherry laughed at Delfi.

"You have eaten more than you have gathered," she exclaimed.

"My basket is full," the little girl protested. "I have as many as any of you."

More than anyone else, Delfi had been changed by the King's power. She was no longer shy or afraid, nor yet bowed down by what her father, Josh, had done in betraying Salvis, although she was still ashamed.

Morwen, always the practical one, sighed deeply. "We should go home. Mother will want us to get the fruit washed and preserved... Petroc, why do you laugh?"

"Home," he replied. "The farm really is our home again. It was worth all our hard work. Father would be so proud of us!"

His remark met with silence. Finally, Morwen said, "We all worked hard, but the King blessed us. He sent us good friends to help and he has made our money last so that we could buy everything we need. And he sent Uncle Amos to us. We should never have been able to do all this on our own."

Petroc scowled. "I do not seek a quarrel, you must have your opinion, but I shall have my own. Let's just rest here for a while. Do you remember the time when Luke and I went to Black Rock Bay and Father was so angry?"

"He had forbidden you to go there," Morwen pointed out. "He said it was dangerous."

"It's not so bad. It was great fun, leaping from one rock to the next."

"Would it have been such great fun if you had fallen into the sea?" Morwen asked, her voice rising angrily.

"Look!" Delfi cut across their argument. "Look, the dolphins are playing again!"

They watched as the dolphins leapt and dived through the surf, their grey bodies glistening silver in the sun.

Suddenly Cherry asked, "What has happened to Bellum? He seems quiet. Do you think he has decided to stay in his castle and leave us alone?"

"Not him," Petroc replied. "He'll be planning something. We should be prepared."

"I did see Esram and Carrik," Morwen told them, "when I went to the village with Mother. Carrik looks just ordinary now. He doesn't wear that serpent thing on his tunic. He spoke to us. He said hello. He just seemed like anyone else, really. I was not afraid of him or Esram either."

A chill crept slowly down Petroc's spine, bringing with it a sense of dread that he could not explain. It was not fear. It was more a feeling that something was coming that he had no power to stop.

"Let's go home," he said abruptly. He pulled Cherry to her feet. "We have to get the fruit prepared."

Amos was splitting logs in the yard just like Tobias used to do. It seemed a lifetime ago. When he saw them coming he stopped, almost as though he had been waiting for them.

"You have a mighty lot of fruit there! Martha will be pleased with you."

"I've worked hard," said Delfi, holding up her basket for inspection. It was full, but it was smaller than the others and Petroc had slipped some of his fruit in with hers, but no-one told her.

"You've done well, child," Amos said. "Now go and show Martha. You will need to get those berries cleaned before supper time because important decisions have to be made today."

He would say no more, no matter how hard Petroc glared at him. In Petroc's eyes, the farm belonged to Martha, Morwen and most of all to himself and as the only man he felt any decisions should be made by him.

It was no use pressing Amos or even Martha. When she was asked, she simply said, "First things first. The fruit will go bad if it is left unwashed. We shall see to that first. When the fruit is preserved we shall have supper and then we shall talk."

So they set to work and soon their shelf was filled with pots of jelly and jam ready for the long, cold months of the season called the Time of Snows.

At last, when supper was eaten, Amos and Martha were ready to talk.

Amos took the lead. "It is time I returned to my own farm," he said carefully. "I must see how my sons have fared without me, and whether our crops are sown. I have asked Raldi to keep an eye on you all, and I shall return in a few days. Meanwhile Petroc, I feel that you and Morwen could plant our seed. The hard work, the ploughing, is done. You must have helped your father with the sowing many times?"

"Yes we have," Petroc said cautiously. "But Uncle, I feel there is more?"

"Yes there is." Amos took a deep breath. "I think Martha should come with me, and Delfi too, and that they should remain with my family on the far side of the island."

Morwen drew in her breath with a sigh that was almost a sob. "Mother, you cannot leave us!"

"Your mother will be more comfortable there during the hard season," Amos explained. "It will be so cold here, and she should not be sleeping on the floor! Where I live is warmer than here. Delfi, the people on the far side of the island will not know who you are. They will not know you are Josh's daughter. Oh yes, I have seen the way they look at you and the way they speak to you in the village. It will be a kinder life for you there."

"I do not care!" Delfi protested. "I want to stay here. This is my family now."

"My family shall be yours," Amos told her. "You will still have Martha to care for you. Delfi, it is for the best. Then, when the Time of Snows is over we shall review the situation. They will return when the time is right."

A tear rolled down Cherry's cheek.

"Martha you have been a mother to me since I have been here. Please do not go."

"I have to." Martha was close to tears herself. "I found our time in the cave house so hard. The damp got through to my bones. The farmhouse will still be cold, although it is not damp. Amos is right. I cannot bear the hardship any more."

"We will get you a bed," Cherry promised desperately. "We will ask Raldi to make you one!"

"It is not just that. If it were, that would be easy to solve. I... I have not been well lately, children. When the King sent the new power, it rolled back the years and it is true that I do feel stronger, but the Time of Snows is coming and the King expects us to be wise. Now I need someone to care for me as in the past I have cared for you."

"We will!" Cherry told her. "We will take it in turns."

It was Petroc who settled things. He knew the right thing to do and he was brave enough to face the truth.

He placed a protective arm around Cherry's shoulders.

"They must go," he said firmly.

Morwen, watching them silently, grew uneasy. Seeing Petroc and Cherry together made her feel left out of their lives. It was as though they had a secret part of themselves which no-one else knew about.

Morwen was jealous.

Chapter 10

The Feathered Thieves

The departure next morning was very subdued.

It was with heavy hearts that Petroc, Morwen and Cherry watched the old cart rumble off across the meadow to make the long journey south to the far side of the island.

Only once Delfi looked back and waved, and then they were gone.

"Well," Morwen said sadly, "now we really are on our own, at least until Uncle Amos returns. Petroc, it seems you must take on his responsibilities. Where do we start?"

"We start," Petroc replied, "by deciding who is to do what. When that is done, then we must lose no time in planting that seed. We can never be sure when the first snows will fall and then it will be too late."

He was so ready with his answer that it was plain that he must have been giving it some thought.

Actually, he had laid awake into the early hours of morning, turning things over in his mind. He did not want his mother to leave, but he admitted that she was not looking well and it was for the best.

He was also determined that the farm would continue to prosper whilst Amos was away.

"Morwen is the best cook," Cherry said quickly. "She should take Martha's place."

Morwen was not happy with that, "You are last here. You have spent your life being a lady's maid. I know the work on the farm. I should be the one to help

Petroc in the fields. And you have a bad leg or foot or whatever it is. That will slow you down."

"It will not!" Cherry protested. "When has my lameness ever kept me from playing my part? I have worked as hard as you and more!"

Petroc, realising that he had to stop a full battle from raging, put a restraining hand on each of their shoulders.

"You shall take turns to cook and clean the house. One day Morwen, the next Cherry."

"What about you?" Morwen was too angry to listen to reason.

Petroc shrugged. "If you think I would be more use cooking than out in the fields, then I must take my turn."

"No… no of course not," Morwen muttered. "You are bigger and stronger than either of us. You should work on the farm as our father did. And today I shall cook and I shall milk the goat and I shall feed the hens."

"Today we plant seeds." Petroc said firmly. "All of us. We can feed the hens first and milk the goat, but then we must all help to sow the seed. We have three bags of seed. That is one each. The three of us should get it done in a day."

"What about supper?" Morwen asked indignantly. She was not at all sure she liked being told what to do by her brother, who was only a year older than herself.

"We have cheese and fruit and bread. That will do for today. Now, the sooner we start, the sooner we shall be done. Morwen, you should do something with your hair."

Morwen gasped in astonishment. Her mouth dropped open. Lately she had taken to wearing her thick hair loose so that it rippled down her back in red-gold waves. She liked it so and thought that Petroc had gone too far.

"You shall not tell me how to do my hair!"

"Morwen, as it is, you will spend all day pushing it out of your eyes. That will take up precious time."

"It would be better to braid it," Cherry agreed. "I'll do it for you, if you like?"

"I can do my own hair, thank you!" Morwen retorted, her face red and tears of humiliation pricking her eyes. "You feed the hens!"

She thought it was unfair of Petroc to tell her what to do and even more unfair of Cherry to take his side.

One day, she thought, I shall prove to both of them that they do not know everything there is to know.

One day soon.

Sowing the seed was the part of farming Petroc liked the most. The prepared ground was the reward for the back-breaking work of clearing the fields and ploughing.

Before this time next year they would have a fine crop of their own to harvest.

They took a field at a time, dividing each into three. That way they could work together and encourage one another. Before long they were laughing as they each tried to finish their section first.

By mid-afternoon the job was done.

"These crops will grow strong," Morwen said as she surveyed the land. "I believe the King will bless our hard work."

Petroc's face darkened. "Our hard work will make the crops grow, not the King. Come on, I'm hungry, even if you two are not. Let's go home."

As they walked across the last field Cherry stopped and pointed to the sky. She gave a shout of fear.

"Look, look! Birds! Crows! Hundreds of them!"

"Oh no," Morwen wailed. "They are going to eat the seed!"

They stood helpless as three frozen statues while the army of black feathered thieves descended on their fields. Within minutes they had been completely stripped of seed.

The girls were standing close together. Cherry was crying.

"What shall we do?" Morwen asked desperately. "I have never seen the birds do that, never before. What made them do it, Petroc? Such things never happened when our father was alive."

Petroc knew that somehow Bellum was responsible for this. He also knew that Carrik, no matter how friendly he might seem, had been furious that the King had given them the farm.

Petroc's response was to stride off in the opposite direction and walk away.

He never knew why his steps led him to Black Rock Bay. Maybe it was because yesterday he was remembering about the time he and Luke had gone there together?

He scrambled down the steep cliff path. He knew that this bay was the most treacherous on this part of Karensa, but he welcomed the danger. He wanted to forget all about caution. How could he have been so stupid as to think that Carrik would simply let them take control of their farm? If the King was as powerful as Morwen and others said, why did he allow Bellum to send the birds?

He ignored the thought that he, Petroc, had refused to give any credit to the King for the way the farm had grown.

He stood on a black shiny rock at the sea's edge. It was as close to the foaming water as he could get. He wanted danger. He wanted to take risks.

"Why?" he shouted at the sea, "Why did you go back home, Luke? Why didn't you stay here with us?"

Then he shouted at the sky.

"Salvis, if you can hear me, do something! Don't just give up and die like you did before! Help me! What am I going to do? We have no more seed! Even if we were to sow more seed, the birds would only eat it again!"

Then he began to leap from rock to rock, defying nature.

"Bellum, you won't bring me down!" he yelled at the top of his voice. "You tried enough times when I was your prisoner but you never did it, and you will not do it now!"

Suddenly, he realised that the rock he was standing on was surrounded by water. The tide must have turned. It was what Tobias had warned him about so long ago.

There was no safe way back to the shore. He would have to leap blindly and hope he landed on a rock, remembering where he thought they were.

Taking hold of his courage, he leapt into the air and landed safely. Then again, only this time his foot slipped and with a loud cry he fell into the sea.

He began to swim but the current carried him, not to the shore but towards the sharp rocks at the bottom of the cliff. The water was over his head and in his eyes. He struggled to the surface and took a deep gulp of air before the sea dragged him under again.

This time as he surfaced, someone took his hand and through the spray, he saw a boy's face surrounded by fair hair.

"Luke?" he gasped incredulously. "Luke, is that you?"

The hand pulled him towards the shore until at last he lay face down on the shingle.

He forced open his eyes.

It was not Luke.

It was Esram who had pulled him from the sea.

Coughing and spluttering, Petroc pulled himself to his hands and knees. He felt very sick.

"Esram, what are you doing here?"

Then he turned away and he really was sick.

Afterwards he felt much better.

He stared up at Esram who was as wet as he was. Clearly he had risked his own life to save Petroc.

"Why did you do that? You hate me. Your uncle wanted our farm. Why didn't you let me drown?"

The other boy gave him a strange look that was hard to understand. If Petroc had not known better he might have thought that Esram wanted to be friends.

"I do not hate you," Esram said flatly.

"Well Carrik does! And you did not treat me well when I was in Bellum's stronghold."

"That was then. Things have changed."

Petroc gave a short laugh. "Oh yes, things have changed. You have no power over me any more."

Esram shrugged. "We should return home. We both need to change our clothes and get dry and warm."

He pulled himself to his feet and headed back up the cliff where his pony stood waiting, leaving Petroc not only feeling weak, but confused.

Chapter 11

Go Forward

For what seemed like a long time, Petroc sat on the grassy cliffs and stared down at the water crashing on the rocks below, the silver spray hissing as the sea thundered nearer and nearer.

If Esram had not arrived, he could so easily have been down there now, washed in like driftwood with the tide. Each time he thought about it, he shuddered.

He had hoped that his clothes would dry out in the sun so that Morwen and Cherry would not have to know what had happened, least of all that he had been rescued by Esram, but they were now many weeks into the Time of Gathering and the sun had lost its full power.

Far out on the rocks by the headland he could hear seals barking as they played in the wild spray. In the old days, each creature had lived in harmony, side by side with people. That was why they had not been ready for the crows to attack and eat their corn. It would not have happened before.

Petroc thought longingly of those days.

"Salvis, you came to fight for the King, so why did you let Bellum kill you?" he said out loud. Just for a second, his pride crumbled. "Salvis!" he shouted out to the sea. "If you really are alive then help us! Help me! What can we do? We have no seed! Next year we shall have no crops to gather in!"

Some of the seals had swum closer and they were sunning themselves on the rocks near the shoreline.

They were barking loudly. For a few brief moments, Petroc felt as though he was at one with them again. They seemed to be telling him to go back to the farm.

Petroc did a little dance of victory, right there on the cliff. The day's lost work did not seem to matter any more. He knew that there was only one way to go and that was forward. It was useless to look back to what was past.

He stood in the doorway of the farmhouse.

"You seem wet," Morwen observed, looking her brother up and down.

Petroc grinned. "I am wet. I fell into the sea. And what do you think? I met some seals at Black Rock Bay."

"Black Rock Bay?" Morwen's face turned red with anger. "You went to Black Rock Bay again? You know how dangerous it is. You deserved to drown."

Petroc continued to grin down at her.

"Don't laugh!" Morwen shouted. "How shall I dry your clothes? You are wet through and through. Oh Petroc, how could you?"

"But it was like the old days when we lived in peace with the animals. It was like that with the seals."

His sister was not impressed. "So? It is more important to get you dry than to stand here talking about seals. Cherry, what are you doing?"

Cherry was rummaging through an old wooden chest which stood by the window. She pulled out three bundles of cloth. The grey one she gave to Petroc. A soft olive green was for Morwen. A dark wine-coloured one she kept for herself.

"What are these?" Morwen still sounded cross.

"They are gifts for us. Your mother gave them to me before she left. She said we were to use them when they were needed. Well, Petroc is wet and you and I are hot and dirty. We need them now."

The bundles turned out to be three new sets of clothes, a tunic and trousers for each of them. Martha must have worked deep into the night to get them finished before she left for the far side of the island.

They decided to try them on and were soon admiring each other; Petroc's tunic was grey, just like Salvis had worn when he stayed with them. Morwen's was soft green that suited the red in her hair and the green in her eyes. Cherry had one of deepest red to show off her dark eyes and rosy cheeks.

Cherry burst into tears; not a few tears trickling down her cheeks, but floods of tears as though her heart would break.

"Cherry, what is it?" Petroc asked, watching helplessly. "Is your colour not right?"

"Of course it is not the colour!" Cherry sobbed. "It is just… just… your mother is so kind. She has treated me as one of her own."

"Yes," Morwen said quietly, "she would," and she went behind the curtain to be alone in her sleeping space.

There, she too started to cry. Then she saw Martha's empty mattress and cried even more. Like Petroc, she too longed for the old days to return, but she knew now that they had gone for ever.

When she was empty of tears she went back to join the others at the table and ate what supper she could. She was ravenously hungry, yet at the same time she found it difficult to take an interest in her food. It was only after they had all finished that Petroc voiced the thought that was in all their minds.

"What shall we do?"

"I have looked in the purse. We still have enough money to replace the seed," said Morwen. "I cannot imagine how it has lasted so long, but it has."

Cherry frowned. "But what is there to stop Bellum sending more birds and the same thing happening again?"

"Do you think Bellum did send them?" asked Morwen, sounding surprised.

"Yes!" chorused Petroc and Cherry.

Petroc went on, "Carrik hates us having the farm, no matter what he pretends. He has probably been watching everything we have been doing. He could easily have asked Bellum to send the birds. Bellum used to be a Lord of the Palace, just like Lord Veritan. He would have that power."

"But…" Morwen chewed her lip thoughtfully. "But Carrik has been friendly."

"He is not as he seems," Petroc told her. "Just because Esram pulled me out of the sea, it does not make him my friend!"

He could have bitten off his tongue.

"Esram?" Cherry exclaimed. "Carrik's nephew, Esram? Esram pulled you out of the sea?"

Morwen was suspicious. "Why didn't you say?"

"This does not get us anywhere." Petroc tried to change the subject. He began to sound pompous. "Sister, I do not know what you must be thinking of. You know well that Carrik and Bellum are our enemies. Did they not kill our own father? You should be thinking more of a plan to help us. What shall we do? We must decide."

Suddenly, as though she had been thinking about it for a while, Cherry got up from the table and went outside into the growing dusk. When she returned she was carrying two long sticks from the wood pile.

Taking a length of twine, she tied them together to form a cross. As Petroc and Morwen watched open-mouthed, she dressed the cross in her old clothes. Finally she took a turnip from the vegetable store and placed it on the top of the cross after first piercing it with the long knife Martha used for preparing food. As a finishing touch she crammed a woollen hat over it.

"There!" she said triumphantly. "To a crow it will look like one of us and when the wind blows, the clothes will flap so that the birds will be too scared to come down on the field."

First of all the others laughed, then they stopped laughing.

"It might just work," said Morwen.

Petroc laughed again. "We could name him Lord Crow Scare."

"Lord Scarecrow," Cherry giggled. "That is his name; Lord Scarecrow of High Field!"

Petroc liked that but Morwen scowled. She felt left out again; no matter how hard she tried to push the thought from her mind, it returned to haunt her like a soft voice whispering in her ear.

'They do not want you any more.'

Before going to bed that night they had made two more scarecrows and had decided that first thing next morning they would all go into the village to replace the wasted seed.

They would need three bags, one for each person to carry. They would lock and bolt the farm and trust that it would be safe until they returned. Then they would have time to get the seeds planted before Amos returned. It would be better than telling their uncle that there was nothing actually in his ploughed fields.

After supper, whilst Petroc brought in fresh logs for the fire, Morwen and Cherry washed the dishes.

Cherry sensed that her friend was unhappy. She thought it was because Morwen did not like their plans.

"I feel this is what the King would want us to do," she said, trying to reassure her.

"Maybe," Morwen turned to put way the platters and by accident she kicked Cherry's bad foot. She was instantly sorry. Morwen was too gentle hearted to want to hurt anyone, no matter how bad she felt herself.

"It will be fine," Cherry gasped, holding the foot in both hands.

"Oh, but I can see it hurts! Cherry… maybe if we went to the King's Palace he would make your foot better?"

"But I have always been lame."

"That is no reason to stay lame. I saw Salvis make sick people well many times while we were all living in the Bay of Dolphins. Once, he made Delfi well."

Cherry was still holding the sore foot.

"Let's sit by the fire. Tell me stories about Salvis."

"You have heard most of them."

"I love to hear them, again and again."

For a short while, Cherry had made Morwen feel better, but as they settled down in front of the blazing logs it was Petroc who Cherry snuggled up against so that Morwen was left on hr own.

Again the voice in her ear whispered that she did not belong any more.

Chapter 12

Only to Look

"Just look at the village!" Morwen exclaimed. "I have never seen the village like this before!"

It seemed as though the entire village was having a party, for it was teeming with people and, even on a day like this, with a grey sky and black clouds that threatened rain, the village square was bright with colour.

As well as the usual fisher-people's stalls selling herring and mackerel, lobsters and crabs, there were many other stalls arranged around the cobbled square. Every trader was shouting his wares at the top of his voice, each trying to outdo the other.

"Buy sweet honey from my own hives!"

"Buy apples and quinces, pears and plums! They are all from my own orchard, ripe and ready to eat!"

"See, ribbons for the ladies! I have fine lace, buttons and bright ribbons!"

Morwen looked longingly at the array of ribbons on this stall. Green ribbons would set off her new clothes and her red hair. Her hand reached up to touch her own plait which had no adornment at all. Martha had always kept her well supplied with hair ribbons but now she was not here.

Petroc guessed what she was thinking. There was nothing his sister liked more than to wash, comb and dress hair, her own or other people's.

"If we have enough money left over when we have bought our seed then you shall both have new ribbons," he promised.

Ruefully Cherry ran her finger through her short, black curls.

"I shall not need ribbons," she said sadly.

"You will," Morwen told her. "Your hair is beginning to grow, and until it does, I have an idea of what we could do with it. Oh, look over there! That man is swallowing fire!"

They stood at the back of the crowd and watched the fire eater.

"How does he not get burnt?" Morwen wondered.

Cherry smiled. "It is a trick. In Bellum's castle, he would often do this."

"You mean he is Bellum's man?"

"He was," Cherry said slowly. "Perhaps he has changed? See, he has ended now and there is the juggler. He was there too, in the castle."

The juggler was followed by acrobats, but before they had finished their display, the children moved away. They had no money to put in the hat that was about to be passed round.

There were other things to see. There was dancing, men and maids, and side shows where for a penny you could knock down some skittles and win a prize.

"Oh, I wish it could always be like this," Morwen sighed. "Why do we have so much work to do and so little enjoyment?"

Petroc and Cherry did not answer. They truth was, they both thought the same. Such pleasures, music and fun and entertainment, could make you forget you problems.

In the centre of the market square a large crowd was gathering and the two girls clamoured to see what was happening. Petroc's shout, that they had work to do, fell on deaf ears.

"It is Carrik!" Cherry gasped. "But he is so changed!"

And those are Lord Bellum's men," said Morwen, "and they too are changed. They no longer look like his followers, do they? What has happened to them all? It must be that Bellum has decided not to be wicked any more?"

Petroc and Cherry could not believe that this was true, but they could not deny that Bellum's household looked different now.

They no longer wore their uniforms of black tabards with the coiled scarlet serpents, the emblem that Bellum had made his own. They were dressed in bright tunics of green, red and gold. They were no longer armed. Not one of them carried a sword.

But it was more than that; they were no longer threatening. Instead they seemed happy and relaxed and set for an enjoyable day out.

Petroc was very uneasy. Terrible memories of what Bellum was capable of were still fresh in his mind.

"It is not so," he muttered. "It cannot be so…"

"Oh Petroc, you are too suspicious! Let us at least hear what Carrik has to say!"

Their old landlord was standing on a raised platform, reading from a scroll. He was dressed in a simple russet tunic and, like the other servants of Bellum's castle he did not carry a sword.

His voice too was not quite the same. It no longer held any threat.

"Good people, you have worked hard and lost much!" he cried. "The war is now over and we must forget our battles and live in peace. To celebrate, and as a token of his good intent, the Lord Bellum invites each of you to a feast in his castle. See, he even provides you with transport to take you there!"

He held up his hand and a cart rumbled across the village square. And what a cart! It was pulled by two horses of purest white and decorated with flowers of every colour. If it should rain, the cart had a roof of what seemed to be gold. The wheels were also gold while the shafts were made of silver. All four corners of the cart were decorated with multi-coloured ribbons of silk and satin.

"Oh look, look!" Morwen laughed excitedly. "Everyone is getting in!"

This was not quite true. Many people were getting in the cart, but many more were doubtful and were turning away.

"There are no guards on the gates of my master's castle," Carrik encouraged them. "It is not like the King's Palace. My master's house is open to any who choose to enter. Come, good people, forget your cares, forget your work for today. Have a holiday! Lord Bellum has a great banquet prepared!"

Morwen clapped her hands. "Brother, we must go!"

Petroc and Cherry stared at her, unable to quite believe what she was saying.

"How can you?" Petroc cried. "How can you even think of it after all we have told you?"

"Morwen, things are not as they would seem," Cherry added. She sounded worried. "We know what Bellum is really like. We have been prisoners in that castle."

As she watched them standing so close together, Morwen felt as though something snapped inside herself. She was tired of them thinking they knew more than she did. She was tired of being made to feel left out of their lives.

"That was before," she argued. "You can see that they are not the same. It cannot be so bad or the butterflies would not have gone there!"

"Butterflies?" Cherry asked bewilderedly.

"We did see some going there," Petroc explained. "But Morwen, you cannot follow a crowd of butterflies!"

Morwen stamped her foot in frustration and temper.

"Yes I can," she said stubbornly. "You keep telling me how you have both been inside Lord Bellum's castle and now I want to see it for myself."

As she saw their dismayed faces, she relented a little. "Look, I will not actually go inside. I just want to look through the gates, that is all, I promise. I know what I am doing. You should not worry about me. I can look after myself."

Before they could stop her, she had pushed to the front of the crowd and climbed into the cart.

Petroc tried his best to follow, but by now the press of the people was so great that he was pushed back, and the last he saw of his sister was a wave of her hand as, followed by many others who could not find room in the cart, the procession left the market square.

Petroc and Cherry stared helplessly after her.

"What shall we do?" Cherry whispered. "Petroc, I feel I am to blame. If I had not joined your family, she would not have felt so left out."

Petroc scowled by way of an answer.

"Should we go after her?" Cherry added.

"We should get the seed for the farm."

"But Morwen... "

"Morwen made her choice. We have come here to buy seed. If we do not sow our crops very soon, the first snows will be here and then we shall be in trouble next year when we have no corn to harvest. And make no mistake, Cherry, I am determined that I will restore my father's farm. It is what he would want and it is what I want to do."

"But Morwen..."

"Morwen is my little sister and she is in danger, I know that. If she is not back by nightfall I shall go after her."

"You would dare to enter that castle again?"

"Yes... if she is not back... but Morwen is not that foolish, Cherry. I do not believe that she will really go to Bellum... Now here is the corn merchant, so let us concern ourselves with the job which we came to do."

However, buying the corn was not so easy. Amos had been able to strike a deal with the corn merchant so that they paid a reasonable price, but the man was not so willing to bargain with two children. In the end they could only afford two bags of seed, not three.

"Oh well," said Petroc, "one each to carry equals one for each field."

"But Morwen..." Cherry said for the third time. "Petroc, I am really scared for her."

"Yes," Petroc said grimly. "So am I."

Chapter 13

A Sea-green Butterfly

The procession wound its way slowly, briefly skirting the Dark Forest, and then across the Meadow of Flowers towards Bellum's castle.

It was led by a group of musicians all dressed in tunics and trousers of bright colours, some with pipes, others with trumpets, some with cymbals and others with drums, harps or lyres.

The people sitting in the cart clapped in time to the music, while others walking behind turned their steps into a dance.

Morwen sat at the back of the cart next to a man and woman with three not very well behaved children; two boys who were squabbling, and a girl who was even worse, so Morwen's attention was divided between the musicians and listening to this family's conversation.

There was hardly time to think about the foolhardy thing she was doing, but even if she had time it would probably have made no difference. She was hurt, she was angry and she was tired of being poor. She was also curious to find out what the castle was really like inside.

It seemed that the mother of the family did not really want to go and was raising all sorts of objections. She had heard bad things about Lord Bellum. The father did not agree.

"It is all only gossip. The children are looking forward to this. We cannot change our minds. It is too late."

It is too late. The words echoed in Morwen's mind. She was suddenly cold

The eldest boy rewarded his father's trust by smacking his sister with his toy flute. She burst into tears. The father slapped the culprit but his hand missed and landed on the wrong boy, so all three children howled in unison.

Morwen thought it was sad. She remembered the happy home where she and Petroc had grown up with loving parents, and she was so thankful for her caring mother and father.

However, she must put her parents out of her mind for she knew only too well what they would say to her now.

How could they understand about Petroc and Cherry making her feel left out? She set her mouth in a hard line. Truly, the farm was all Petroc cared about now.

By now they had crossed the Meadow of Flowers and Bellum's castle towered above them, yet it did not seem to look as dark as before.

Just as Carrik had told them, there was no guard set on the gates, so they clattered across the wooden bridge into the courtyard. The castle now had a moat and she shivered as she looked down on it from the cart, because the water appeared to be unusually black and cold.

The people gazed around in wonder, and now Morwen had to remind herself of her promise not to go right inside the castle. She would just peep inside the door to see what it was like and then she would slip away unseen.

To her horror, as the last of the followers danced through the gates, the iron portcullis dropped down behind them.

A chill of fear gripped Morwen's heart. She refused to own up to it. She told herself that Bellum had probably shut the gates because the castle would not have room for any more guests. Then she regarded the vastness of the building and knew this was not true. It was big enough to accommodate every person on Karensa if they wanted to go there.

Maybe there were wolves around, then? Or bears? Whatever the reason, now that she was here she may as well look around. She was not going to come all this way for nothing and besides, she did not want to go home too early because that would not give Petroc and Cherry enough time to get really worried. Morwen wanted them to worry.

They were in a square courtyard surrounded on all sides by walls of grey stone. In the centre of the courtyard was a high platform.

Morwen felt a little sick. Was this where Salvis had died? Surely not, for it was an ordinary platform which today was draped with silk banners of red and gold.

Quickly, Morwen tried to forget the image of Salvis' kind face in her mind.

Carrik climbed up the steps to the stage.

"Welcome, welcome to you all! Lord Bellum will greet you soon, but for now you must come, come inside. Tonight we have a great feast prepared. We have declared today a holiday for all."

Eagerly they climbed down from the cart, each anxious to be the first inside this splendid place. Morwen let the quarrelling family go first, so she was the very last to get down. As she stepped from the cart, she lost her footing and stumbled, for the cart was very high and there was no-one left to help her.

A hand took hers and when she looked up to thank the kind person, she looked into Lord Bellum's eyes.

Morwen pulled back, but today Bellum was smiling, not his customary mocking sneer but a smile that seemed warm and almost caring.

He was changed. Gone was the armour and black silken clothes. Gone was the sword and shield. He was still dressed finely but today he wore blue and silver, which were Lord Veritan's colours. He held Morwen's hand long after she had recovered her balance.

"Little Morwen, is it not?" he said softly. "You see, child, I was right. Did I not say that one day soon you would walk into my castle of your own free will?"

"I… I… I cannot stay," she stammered. "I promised my… my brother, I would be home…"

Bellum laughed. His laughter was filled with music.

"You know very well that Petroc is concerned only for Cherry," he murmured in her ear.

Morwen felt her colour rise with shame to think that even Lord Bellum understood how she was feeling.

In spite of all her fears, Morwen was curious, and like one asleep she allowed herself to be led by Lord Bellum into the shadows of the very castle where she had promised not to go.

It was beautiful!

The scene took her breath away. As they passed through the huge oak door they were in a great hall, bigger than Morwen could ever have imagined. This hall was pillared and vaulted and hung with drapes of all colours that reflected dimly in the black, marbled floor. Flowers and vines were wound around each pillar.

At one end of the hall and down two sides, were tables heavily laden with food, while in the centre part, many people stood talking and laughing, all dressed in rich velvets and silks and furs.

Morwen noticed that only the men wore tunics and trousers. The ladies were dressed in a fashion she had never seen before. They did not wear trousers, but strange gowns that reached to the floor. Their hair was loose and dressed with sparkling jewels.

Morwen looked down at her own simple clothes and knew that the green wool was drab by comparison. She felt like a caterpillar in a room full of butterflies.

Bellum placed a jewelled finger beneath her chin and this time she did not shrink from him. He snapped his fingers and two servant girls came running and bowed down before him to the floor.

He motioned to them to rise. "You know what you have to do," he said. He did not use the same soft tones to them that he had used to Morwen. His voice now was harsh.

"This maid is to sit at my table tonight. See that she is suitably attired. And see you do it well, or you will answer to me."

The two girls scrambled to their feet and gestured to Morwen to follow them across the hall and up a flight of winding stone stairs.

They led her round and round the winding steps until they came to a small turret room. At first Morwen was scared they were going to lock her inside, all her old fear of Lord Bellum returning. But no, they came in with her and there was nothing to fear. It was a bedroom, at one end of which was a marbled bath of warm, scented water.

The taller of the girls gestured to the bath.

"Please?" she said. She seemed nervous. Morwen could not think why she would be nervous of her.

"You mean I must get in there?" she asked, swallowing hard. Many times she had bathed in the ocean but she had never had a bath before.

"Yes. Take off your clothes. Come, mistress, you are safe. There is only you here and no-one will enter. Please, do not take too long. Our master desires to see you at supper."

Morwen rather liked being called mistress. It made her forget she was poor and it definitely made her forget that she was only twelve years old.

So she lay back in the warm bath and let the girls wash and perfume and later dry her long hair.

Afterwards, she reached for her old clothes but the same girl pushed her hand away.

"They will not do at all, mistress," she said. From a wardrobe she took a gown of green silk. She slipped it over Morwen's head and laced it up. Then she dressed her hair.

At last, after what seemed like an eternity, she motioned to the smaller girl, who brought out a full length mirror of polished glass.

Morwen's heart raced when she saw her reflection in the glass. The farm girl was gone. The child was gone. In her place was a fine maiden, even a princess, and yes, the rock pool had not lied that day on the beach. Her face was fair.

The caterpillar peasant child was gone and a lovely sea-green butterfly had emerged.

The gown felt strange, but it looked well on her and the colour was like nothing Morwen had ever seen, a sea-green silk shot with silver. The bodice had long, narrow sleeves and was laced tightly down to the high waist. From there the garment fell in graceful folds to her feet which were clad, not in boots, but in soft, velvet slippers. Her hair was left loose, held only by a green ribbon.

Wonderingly she held out the skirts of the gown in front of the mirror and found that with every movement they reflected a different shade, which made her think of all the moods of the ocean.

"Oh," she breathed. "Oh, it is so beautiful. I had never thought to wear anything so beautiful. Thank you so much."

"Do not thank us, thank Lord Bellum," the smaller girl told her. "And mistress… please, take care…"

The taller girl flashed her companion a warning glance. "Lord Bellum has many such lovely things," she said.

Just as she spoke, there was a tap on the door.

"That will be your escort for the feast. Shall we let him in, mistress? And yes, you do look beautiful."

Morwen nodded her agreement, not knowing what to expect. She certainly did not expect to see this tall, fair-haired youth, dressed from head to toe in cloth of silver.

"Esram!" gasped Morwen

Chapter 14

Castle of Shadows

As Esram stared down at her, Morwen giggled nervously. Her new clothes felt strange, but another glance in the mirror reassured her that they did not look strange at all.

Esram held out his hand and she placed her own hand in his. She was surprised by how soft and white his hands were, but then, he had never had to pull a plough or weed a field. She was very aware that her own hands were brown and freckled and roughened by farm work.

He made no comment, but led the way down the stairs and back into the Great Hall.

They stood together in the doorway, taking in the scene that met their eyes. The hall was a blaze of colour and now, with evening falling, it was lit by many torches, their flames flickering and dancing and making the colours seem even brighter than they really were. The long table at the top of the hall and the other tables leading from it down the two sides were each set with gold platters and goblets and each table was already piled high with food. There were jugglers and acrobats - the ones Morwen had seen in the village square - and even now the guests were taking their seats at the tables.

Morwen pulled Esram to a seat near the door where they would not be noticed, but Esram held her back.

"No, we are to sit at Lord Bellum's table tonight," he said. "It is our master's own command and it is well to obey him."

Morwen experienced a small shiver of unease, but she again pushed it away and followed Esram to their places at the high table, on the left of a massive, throne-like chair. Carrik was sitting on a smaller chair on the right.

As they took their seats there was a loud fanfare of trumpets and at once everyone rose to their feet, as Bellum and his entourage came into the hall.

Morwen's knees began to shake. If only she could have sat where no-one could see her! Yet, part of her was enjoying herself; the new clothes and the feeling of being grown up and important. Her heart began to thump with excitement and her eyes had a new sparkle. There was something exciting and dangerous about Bellum; something she did not yet understand, but something which made her want to know more.

If he had seemed splendid before, then he was even more so now.

He could not have found his crown, for his head was bare, but in spite of that he looked in every part a king.

This evening he was dressed from head to foot in black and gold. However, Bellum's gold had no real lustre; it was dull, almost like a false gold, as if it needed to be polished to make it shine.

But Lord Bellum was magnificent and as he took his seat on his throne and indicated that all should be seated too, he smiled at Morwen and Esram. His teeth were very white and his eyes gleamed, sometimes black, sometimes amber in the torchlight.

"Little Morwen, so you stayed after all," he said, still smiling.

Morwen met his gaze. The farm and Petroc and Cherry seemed a thousand miles away, and her new clothes had given her boldness. She was no longer afraid.

"Yes, I am still here, my lord," she replied.

"That is well! That is very well. You make a fine couple, you and Lord Esram. He has a promising future in my household when he is grown up. His uncle, Lord Carrik, has served me well."

Carrik, seated on the other side of him, saluted her. A small voice in her heart said, *'this man killed your father,'* but she deliberately chose not to listen.

Lord Bellum was still speaking. "You see, Morwen, I was right, you are passing fair, and when you are grown to a young woman you will grace my court with Esram."

Morwen felt her face burning and Esram also looked embarrassed by his obvious meaning.

She had no time to dwell on it, for supper was now served and she had never seen food like this in all her days. There was every meat and fish she could think of; fruit piled high on dishes of gold and some food she had never even seen before. There were many different kinds of bread and spicy sauces, a tempting variety of desserts too. The wine was so plentiful that it flowed like water.

Morwen had never drunk wine before. She took a sip from her golden goblet. The red liquid was rich and sweet and so she drank some more.

She was annoyed when a picture of her brother and Cherry flashed across her mind. She remembered that once they had been prisoners here and made to eat scraps from the table at banquets like this. On such an occasion Bellum had told Petroc that their father had died and had been horribly cruel in the telling.

As though reading her mind, Lord Bellum whispered, "Your brother could have had this too, my dear, if he had desired it," and she comforted herself that this, at least, was probably true.

All through the long banquet the musicians played for them, and all through the banquet Morwen sipped at the wine in her golden goblet. When they had finished eating, Carrik stood up and raised his goblet high.

"A health to Lord Bellum, the true ruler of Karensa!"

Morwen stood up with the others and was shocked when the room spun round.

"You have taken too much wine," Esram hissed in her ear. "Come, you must drink a toast to Lord Bellum. Hold on to my arm and raise your goblet."

She stared at the wine in her hand. To be made into a fine lady and taken to a banquet was one thing; to deny the King was something quite different.

"Oh, I cannot," she murmured, aware than many people were staring at her, including Lord Bellum himself who did not look pleased.

"You must," Esram whispered. "If you do not, Lord Bellum will be angry. Look, pretend."

He took the wine from her and held it to her lips. She tried not to drink it but as he tipped the goblet, either she must drink it or she must let it spill on her new gown. She drank the wine. Lord Bellum appeared to be satisfied. Morwen felt terrible.

Carrik spoke again. "May we ask one more thing of you, Lord Bellum? Would you sing for us? None in all of Karensa has so great a gift in making music to touch the soul."

Bellum smiled. He had obviously been waiting to be asked, and as the musicians played he sang, soft and low, a haunting melody that made Morwen want to cry. She forgot that this man was her enemy and the enemy of the King and of Salvis. She forgot everything except the beautiful notes that filled her heart.

When the song was ended, even Bellum looked sad. With a shock, Morwen realised that there were tears in his eyes and, for a brief moment, she felt sorry for him.

"What is it, my lord?"

"Ah, nothing, little Morwen, nothing," he said so quietly that only she could hear. "Except that with this very song I once ministered to the King…" his voice trailed away.

Curious again, she asked, "Then why did you… why…"

"Why did I disobey the King?" Bellum smiled wryly. "Why indeed? But you see, little one, the King took away the worship that should have been mine."

"But… but he is the King!"

Without any warning, Bellum grew angry and Morwen was afraid she had said too much.

"He is king for now, but not for ever. One day I shall…" Then he seemed to remember that this was a celebration. "Dancing!" he called. "We shall have dancing! The children must take the lead! I once promised little Morwen she should dance."

"I cannot! I cannot dance. I have never learnt."

"Then I shall teach you," Esram said firmly. "It is easy. All you need to do is follow me," and as the music played, he took her hands and led her into the centre of the hall.

He was a good teacher, and soon she knew the steps and began to enjoy herself.

After a time she began to feel light headed again.

"You should not have drunk so much wine," Esram said with unusual concern.

"I… I did not know it would do this to me…"

He led her away from the dancing. "Come, you need some fresh air, then you will feel better. Besides, I have something to show you."

The night air was cool to their cheeks and Morwen's head cleared as Esram led the way across the courtyard and then through another door.

She gasped with delight. "Oh Esram, it is so lovely!"

"I knew you would like it," he said, and his eyes and his voice told her that he was trying desperately to please her.

"So this is where the butterflies came," she breathed.

They were in a long, low room with many windows. The room was filled with green plants, palms and ferns and other foliage that grew on the island of Karensa. The roof of the building was made of glass so that people might almost think they were not in a room at all. Amidst the greenery fluttered butterflies of every colour.

Morwen walked between the plants and as she did so, the butterflies' wings were like music to her ears. Just as before, she had never heard such a sad song, sadder even than the music Bellum had made.

She began to cry.

"What is it, Morwen? You should not be sad. I thought you would like this place?" Esram sounded dismayed.

"It is the butterflies," she sobbed. "I know they want to be free."

Then she understood. She was no different from these butterflies. She was a prisoner like them in this place where even the gold had no shine.

Well, at least she could help them before it was too late. She ran to the nearest window and twisted the catch, opening it wide. Then she opened the next window, then the next.

"Butterflies, leave while you may!" she cried, and in spite of Esram's frantic attempts to stop her, the butterflies took their chance to escape. Soon, all that was left in the room were themselves and the green plants.

"What have you done?" Esram groaned. "Oh, Morwen, what have you done? What will Lord Bellum say? He was collecting those butterflies. He will never forgive you."

"I do not care!" she shouted as the truth flooded into her heart. "I have been foolish! I will never serve Bellum! Never in a thousand years! This castle is not real! The King's castle is real! This is a copy, the Castle of Shadows!"

Her heart was thumping and the room spinning as the wine and the moment overtook her and Esram caught her as she fell.

Chapter 15

Deny Your Fear

Petroc and Cherry walked home in silence. Petroc was too angry and afraid for his sister to eat much at all and Cherry's arms and back ached from carrying the heavy corn seed.

Her foot hurt too. It had been more painful than ever since they had begun to restore the farm because she had very little time to rest. But it was not in her nature to complain. She was glad of a place to call home and if the work was hard, then she would endure it.

She had become very close to Petroc, although she often thought about her former mistress, Zena, who had been so kind. Tas, Zena and Nolis were still living in Bellum's castle and she knew that Zena was unhappy there.

Just like Petroc, she too was worried about Morwen. She had promised not to actually go inside Bellum's castle but that might not have been so easy when the time came.

Petroc's face was white. He felt as though he was in a battle. On one hand his sister was in danger and he should have gone after her and brought her back, but on the other hand his farm was in danger too. They had to get the seed sown if next year they were not to starve. He told himself again and again that this would have been his father's desire.

Privately Cherry thought that Tobias would have put his daughter first, but she did not dare say so.

When finally they rounded the last bend in the path and saw the farm and saw that Josh's old cart was standing outside the farmhouse door, Cherry uttered a cry of relief.

"Petroc, it is your uncle! It is Amos, come back already. We shall be safe now. He will know just what to do."

Petroc did not answer her. *'Morwen is still not safe though,'* he thought.

"Amos, Amos we are so pleased you are home!" she panted as they staggered through the door and thankfully put down the two heavy bags they were carrying.

Amos replaced the lid on the cooking pot he had been stirring.

"So what is this?" he pointed to the corn seed. "Why was the seed not sown yesterday as I asked? And why are there only two bags, not three? And where is Morwen?"

Suddenly, Petroc and Cherry were both exhausted. They had worked so hard, they had walked so far. They both felt as though they had failed, that in some way they had let Amos down.

While they rested on the hard wooden bench, Petroc told his uncle all that had happened while he had been away, with Cherry joining in with the occasional 'yes' or 'that's right.'

When they had finished, Amos nodded thoughtfully. "I did feel that something was wrong. That is why I came back so early. Your mother and Delfi are both settled in their new home and my own land is being well cared for by my sons, so I felt I should come back here."

"You are a good man, Uncle Amos," Petroc told him with a sudden rush of gratitude. "Without you, we should not have survived."

"Yes you would, Petroc," his uncle replied, "because you are the son of Tobias. Morwen is the daughter of Martha, my sister. She, too, will survive. Her loyalty to the King will carry her through. If she is not back before dark, then we must go after her. But first we shall eat this meal. We are all hungry and not able to work without food."

"You do not realise the wickedness of Lord Bellum," argued Petroc, but keeping his voice low. "Morwen might not be free to come home, even if she wants to."

"Then we shall fetch her!" Amos shouted. "But for now, boy, let us eat this meal!"

He began to fill their wooden dishes with stew. All at once the children realised how hungry they were and ate greedily.

Just as they finished, there came a knock on the door. Cherry moved to answer it but Amos pulled her back.

"No, let me go," he told her.

Petroc knew then that in spite of his brave words, Amos was as uneasy as he was himself.

They need not have worried. Standing in the doorway were Raldi, the carpenter, and Daris, the farmer.

"We had a feeling you might be in trouble and we have come to help," Raldi said simply.

This made Petroc feel uneasy. Since that first night when they said the King had given them a new power, it was as though they sensed each other's needs. Petroc had not been there so he had missed whatever it was that happened.

"The King must have sent that thought to you," Amos replied, "for truly we are in need of your help."

He told them the story. "If we all worked hard we could be finished by bed time. And this time our three new friends will help keep the seed safe." He pointed to the three scarecrows the children had made the day before. One was wearing Morwen's old clothes and Cherry struggled hard not to cry.

"They are a good idea," Daris said. "I have been farming all my life and I have never known birds to steal our seed before. They have always been content to eat berries from the hedgerows."

"They were sent by Lord Bellum, I know it," said Cherry. She turned to Petroc. "I feel Carrik desires to once again own your farm. He will not stop until he gets it. Now he has Morwen in his power."

With everyone helping, the work was done must faster and it did not seem too long before the three scarecrows stood like guardians over the newly sown fields. As the old clothes caught the breeze they flapped loudly, so the few birds that came to see what was going on soon flew away, scared at something they did not understand.

Raldi and Daris went home and Amos left the fields soon after that, but Petroc and Cherry hung back, even though it was getting dark early, a reminder that the Time of Snows would soon be here.

"We should go too," said Cherry. She was thinking about Morwen. What was she doing? How was she being treated? Cherry knew only too well that neither Bellum nor Carrik could be trusted, and neither could that trouble-maker Esram, even if he had pulled Petroc from the sea.

As they stood wondering what to do, they saw a bright cloud coming towards them, its pastel colours reflecting the fading sun.

"Oh Petroc, it is the butterflies!" Cherry laughed, clapping her hands together with delight. "You told me about them. See how lovely they are!"

They stood perfectly still for fear of crushing the gentle creatures as they flew all around them, just as they had flown around Petroc and Morwen on the day they had met Lord Veritan in the Meadow of Flowers.

Cherry laughed again. "Their wings sound like music, wonderful music!" Her laughter died. "But it is a sad song! I believe they sing of danger and fear."

"They must have come from Bellum's castle. They could have seen Morwen."

"I know Morwen is not safe, Petroc. I know it! I feel it! Petroc, why did she go there?"

Petroc knew why. He had been feeling guilty all day. He knew that his sister was jealous of his friendship with Cherry.

"I shall go to Bellum's stronghold," he declared, yet even as he spoke, a shiver of dread chilled his spirit. He was very afraid.

"Morwen has become like a sister to me," Cherry told him. "She has been a true friend. I shall come with you."

Petroc would have liked to refuse her help, but he was honest enough with himself to admit that he would need her support, even though she, too, would be afraid.

As the butterflies drifted away, she whispered in his ear, so softly that only he could understand.

"Petroc we shall be together and we shall be brave. We shall help each other. It is time to overcome the past and to deny your fear."

Chapter 16

Who the Son Sets Free...

Morwen struggled to open her eyes. She was so cold. Her head hurt and as she sat up, she realised that she had no idea where she was or how she had got there.

The room was small and square, with a high window which would barely let in any light, even in daytime. There were bars at the window and the walls and floor were stone. The heavy door was locked and bolted.

It was a prison. Tears welled in her eyes and she did not try to hold them back, but let them pour down her cheeks. How could she have been so foolish? She had betrayed Petroc. She had betrayed her father, who had died for the King. She had betrayed Salvis. And worst of all, she had betrayed the King himself by drinking the health of his enemy.

Of her own free will, she had walked into Bellum's stronghold. It had been easy. Her wounded pride, the fine clothes, the rich food and the admiration of others had all made it so easy. She knew it would not be as easy to get out.

Trembling with cold and fear, she stood up and looked around. She could not escape. She might never see her family or the farm ever again. Bellum might have put her here to starve. There was not even a blanket, and the thin silk clothes she wore did not protect her from the damp stone walls.

As her head cleared, she realised there were chains on her wrists, and with that discovery she dropped to her knees and began to cry as never before. Her body shook as she sobbed from deep within her heart, calling first to Petroc, then to Tobias, then to Luke. None of these could help her.

At last she called to the person she had loved more than any; she called to Salvis, the King's son.

"Salvis, I am sorry, I am so sorry! I betrayed you! I was jealous of Cherry! I know I did wrong, Salvis, please forgive me. Please help me!"

When she called his name, her tears stopped and just as he had on that first night at the farm, the King sent his power. It flowed through her in a waterfall of peace.

Morwen never knew how long she knelt there on the hard stone floor, just thinking about Salvis and all the wonderful things he did when they all lived in the Bay of Dolphins.

That was how Esram found her when be unlocked the cell door.

The flames from Esram's torch illuminated the cell with a flickering light.

What he saw left him speechless. He had expected to see Morwen broken and pleading to be set free, but instead her face was filled with radiant joy.

Puzzled, he stepped into the cell and shut the door behind him, resting the torch in an iron clamp on the wall. He knew there was something different in the room, something that he did not understand, something that he had never met before, but something that he desperately wanted for himself.

He knelt down beside her on the dirty floor. He knew too that he could never hurt her.

"Morwen," he said, with a strange new tenderness. "Morwen, do you know why I have come here?"

She turned her head towards him. Her eyes were brighter than any eyes he had ever seen.

"It must be to take me to Lord Bellum?"

Esram nodded. "He is very angry about the butterflies, Morwen. You know you will be punished, even... even worse?"

To his astonishment she smiled at him.

"Then I am ready," she said simply, knowing now that nothing mattered except that Salvis was her friend.

Esram was struggling. His heart was telling him that he needed to have this new thing for himself, but his mind was saying that if he did have it, he would lose all that seemed important to him.

Suddenly she said, "Esram, you feel it too! You want the King to put peace in your heart too!"

"The King will not want me! I've done terrible things."

"Yes, yes he would! As long as you are really sorry and tell him so, the King will forgive you and give you a fresh start."

Esram looked at her. She had nothing. She was a prisoner in chains. Yet she had everything in the world.

All at once his resolve crumbled, and there, on the damp, cold floor of the cell, he gave his life over to the King and for the first time ever he received the special kind of peace brought when the King's love and power filled his heart.

"I have never felt like this before!" he gasped. "It... it's wonderful, it's the most wonderful thing..."

Morwen seemed even happier than he was. "We must go," she said. "Lord Bellum will be waiting."

"I cannot take you there now! I can no longer serve Bellum. We must escape together."

"How?" she asked, practical as ever. "There is no way out of Bellum's stronghold, only... only..." a thought was coming to the back of her mind. "There is only one way," she said slowly. "We can only escape by trusting in Salvis."

Esram was not at all sure. "Well, at least I can get you out of this cell. But after that…"

"Salvis will help us," Morwen said confidently. "He has set us both free. If the King's son has set us free then we really are free and there is no such thing as failure."

In the gathering darkness, Petroc and Cherry crossed the Meadow of Flowers. When they reached the place where Lord Bellum had lost his crown, they stopped. The gloomy walls of the stronghold towered above them. Music and laughter reached their ears and they felt a chill of dread for they knew that the noise meant the feast was still going on.

They also knew that when Bellum's banquets went on long into the night, he would be entertained by tormenting those servants who had upset him that day. Cherry had usually managed to keep out of trouble and escape his attention, but Petroc was summoned many times.

Now, at the thought of going inside the castle, all those terrible memories flooded back to him. They each admitted their fear to themselves, but not to each other.

"Wait," said Cherry. "It will help us if we stop for a little while and concentrate on Lord Salvis."

Petroc sighed impatiently. "What good can that do?"

Even as he spoke, he sensed that they were no longer alone. Slowly, he turned his head and saw that once again, Lord Veritan was standing behind them.

Veritan looked long and hard at Petroc until the boy lowered his eyes, unable to meet his searching gaze.

"Petroc, son of Tobias, why do you not ask the King for help? Why are you so proud?"

Petroc looked at his feet. He knew his face was red.

"Well Petroc, even though you have not asked, the King is aware of your need. I have come to help you."

"Lord, there is only one of you," Cherry said nervously, "but there are many in Bellum's stronghold."

"One Lord of the Palace is a match for a thousand," Veritan told them quite sternly. "Even so, I cannot enter Bellum's house any more than he is able to enter the King's Palace."

Cherry looked at Petroc. His face was scornful. She knew that he was thinking that when it came to a fight Veritan was no more use than Salvis had been.

"What shall we do then, lord?" she asked.

"Petroc, you must learn to trust the King," Veritan said, almost angrily. "Do you think the King, who sent his own son to die in your place, would forsake you now?"

"I know he would never leave us or forsake us," Cherry answered quietly.

"No, he would not, and I am going to help you even though I cannot enter the castle."

Esram led Morwen along a dark, narrow tunnel, only just high enough for them to stand upright. A grown man would have to bend double. It stank of death and decay.

Morwen shuddered. "What is this used for, Esram?"

"You are best not to know."

In spite of her renewed love for Salvis, she was afraid. The King did not banish all fear; he gave strength to overcome it. How could she be sure that

Esram was helping her and not leading her into a trap of his own?

Then, she felt him squeeze her hand and she sensed the King's love in his touch. "Where does this lead, Esram?" she whispered.

"Ssh! You will see. You have to trust me."

Morwen had no choice. They came to a small door and Esram pushed this open, just wide enough to see out.

"Come. No-one is there. It is safe."

She held back. "There must be soldiers. Surely they would not leave any door unguarded?"

"They would this one!"

"Why?" Morwen's fear increased. "Esram, what is this passage used for?"

Esram sighed resignedly. "Sometimes Bellum's prisoners die. Sometimes he has them killed. Sometimes they become sick and any who touch them may become sick too…"

"You mean there is sickness here that takes lives?"

"Not in your cell. That is clean. But this is the way the bodies are taken from the castle for burial. We have to get out of here. We have to take the risk. There is no other way. Morwen, because if Bellum finds you he will show you no mercy, or to me either now that I have helped you."

"But I only freed the butterflies! That is not so bad?"

"Oh yes it is! You do nothing, nothing to go against Lord Bellum."

"But outside, there must be people about. How shall we get out of the castle and across the moat?"

"One step at a time," said Esram. The truth was, he did not know what they were going to do.

"Morwen, we have to go!"

The urgency in his voice convinced her at last that there really was no other way, so they crept out into the growing darkness.

All was quiet. The night air was heady after the stench of the passage. They were at the back of the castle, so, keeping well within the shadow of the castle walls, they moved quickly round towards the gate.

At the very first corner, they sensed danger as they heard the sound of marching feet.

"I said there would be guards!" Morwen whispered with panic rising in her heart.

"Quick – in here!" He took her arm and roughly pulled her through a wooden door, shutting it behind them.

They were in a barn-like place with a small cart of hay and a tired-looking brown horse in a stable. Without ceremony, Esram picked her up and threw her on the cart, covering her completely in straw.

Morwen did not need to ask what the cart was used for. It would be the way dead prisoners left the castle.

"Keep still and be quiet!" he hissed tersely.

The footsteps stopped at the door and Esram slipped outside. She heard him speak to the guards. There was loud laughter. It was horrible; mocking and cruel.

"If that maiden knew what Lord Bellum has planned for her, she would die first of fear," shouted a man's voice.

Esram laughed too, and said, "Your duty is finished now. You must come and watch. I am on my way to fetch the maid from the cells. Shall I warn her of what is in store for her?"

"No, let it be a surprise! We shall enjoy it more!"

There was more laughter and then the sound of marching feet and Esram went back inside the barn and very gently helped Morwen to sit up.

"They have gone. And this has given me an idea. The new guard will not be aware of what has happened tonight, because they would not be allowed to join in the feast. If you hide in the cart I should be able to drive straight cross the drawbridge. They will think…"

Morwen pulled straw from her mouth.

"They will think I am a dead prisoner," she finished for him. "Esram, is that really the only way?"

"I believe so."

She held out her hands. "At least free me from these chains first? They are hurting me. My wrists are bleeding."

"We do not have time. We must go now or not at all."

Even as he spoke he was harnessing the horse to the cart. Then he made her lie down and covered her from head to foot with a heavy blanket.

It was very dark beneath the blanket. Her heart was banging so hard she thought she would be heard. All she could do was to cry silently to Salvis.

Salvis, please help me. Please…

The cart rumbled away and then stopped. Once again she heard laughter, the same cruel laughter.

"Ho, Esram, not another dead?"

"Only one little one!"

"Let me see."

Morwen stopped breathing for what seemed like an eternity until she heard Esram call back.

"Not this time, friend. This one's sickly from top to toe!"

"Best go then. We do not want to catch it!"

Morwen clearly heard the sound of the drawbridge being lowered and the cart rocked from side to side as it moved on to the wooden planks.

Please Salvis, please… please…

They must have been half-way across the bridge when a roar like an angry bull reached their ears.

Bellum had discovered that Morwen was missing from her cell.

"You dare to defy me?" he bellowed. "Esram, come back here and bring that maid! Do as I say! Guard, stop them. Raise the drawbridge!"

The bridge tilted upwards. The frightened horse reared. The cart jolted back. Morwen heard a roaring in her ears as it overturned and both she and Esram were thrown into the icy, black water of the moat.

****

Morwen's breath was forced from her lungs by the sudden cold and shock. She tried to swim, but her long skirts and the heavy chains pulled her down beneath the water.

As she began to lose consciousness, strong arms were beneath her. Her head was lifted above the water and Esram swam for them both until they reached the other side.

Eager hands helped pull them out. They lay still for a few minutes, oblivious even to Bellum's roaring, and when they opened their eyes it was to see Petroc and Cherry, bending over hem.

They were helped to their feet and first Cherry then Petroc gave Morwen a hug. She was shocked to see tears in Petroc's eyes.

"Esram helped me escape. He has joined the King's people."

Petroc nodded, not sure of what to believe.

"You seem to be for ever pulling one of us out of the water, Esram. We are in your debt."

"Look!" cried Cherry. "Look at Lord Veritan!"

The drawbridge had been lowered again and Bellum stood ready to cross, but Veritan, mighty Lord of the Palace, was standing facing him. Veritan's golden sword was drawn and he was swinging it from side to side in a glorious display of flashing light. Bellum could roar all he liked, but there was no way he could pass by him.

Veritan called mockingly to his enemy.

"Bellum, yet another failure! You will never defeat the King!"

"You have no right on my land, Veritan!" Now Bellum's voice revealed his hatred.

"I have not been on your land," Veritan laughed. "I did not need to. You could not even get the better of two children!"

Bellum's voice changed again and he now sounded like a hissing snake.

"Then go, all of you! But mark me I have not finished with them yet. I will not be defied by anyone."

With that he turned and stormed back inside the castle.

In the sudden, unexpected silence, Petroc hugged his sister and for the first time noticed her appearance.

"Morwen, what in the world are you wearing? What have they done to you? How could they put you in chains?"

As the words left his mouth, without anyone moving, Morwen's chains fell away of their own accord. No-one touched them.

The four children looked at each other in disbelief and Morwen stared down at her hands.

"It must be Salvis," she whispered. "Salvis has set me free. Look, look over there!"

In a flash of light they thought they saw a tall, slim man dressed in grey standing a little way from them. As they watched, he waved his hand and was gone. They knew it was Salvis; even Esram knew it.

Now that Bellum had gone back into the castle, Veritan came over to them.

"Do not be afraid, little ones. The King's power is greater than Bellum's can ever be. The King is a giant and Bellum is a worm. Just a worm! Petroc, you did not have to go inside the castle, but you were willing to go. Trust in the King and then Bellum cannot hurt you."

Veritan left quickly for his work was done. Laughing and crying and too exhausted to talk, they started to make their way across the Meadow of Flowers into the safety of the Dark Forest and home.

Chapter 17

...is Free Indeed

The light of first dawn filtered through the shutters of the farmhouse windows when Petroc woke up the next morning.

Next to him, Esram was still asleep and snoring loudly. Petroc frowned. He was still not sure if Carrik's nephew was really a friend.

Amos was not here. He must have got up early. Quietly, so he did not disturb Esram, Petroc slipped out from between the hay and the covering of furs that were his bed. His bare feet touched the cold stone floor and, shivering as he picked up his boots, he tiptoed away.

Once outside the house, he pulled on his boots. Amos was standing at the farm gate staring over the fields which were now sown with good corn. A low mist hung over the ground and over the distant hills and there was a cold chill in the air. The Time of Snows would soon be here.

His uncle did not turn round but continued to stare ahead at the land as Petroc joined him.

"You know that Carrik will not let things rest here?" Amos said quietly.

"Yes," Petroc agreed. "That is what I want to talk to you about. Uncle Amos, do you think that Esram is really loyal to the King?"

"Yes... yes, I do... I am sure that he now has the King's power within his heart."

"Oh, the King, the King," Petroc cried. "It is bad enough that the girls talk in this way but I had thought better of you. You are a grown-up, Uncle Amos. You must see this is only a children's tale?"

Amos said nothing. He did not have to. Petroc had always been taught to respect his elders.

"I should not have been rude to you, I'm sorry for that," he said, but he did not sound very sorry. "You are my mother's brother and she would not like me to be so rude... But I am more interested in protecting the farm than in the King's peace or the King's power or whatever it is called!"

"Maybe," Amos said mildly, "the King's power is what we need to protect the farm? As for Esram, the only danger he brings to us is from his uncle, Carrik. He will have his heart set on revenge. Come, let us walk before breakfast."

They strode off together, the big, red-haired man with the loud voice and the tall, red-haired boy who was so quiet; of the same family, yet with such different ways.

Amos led the way to High Hill and as they walked, they spoke of family matters, of Tobias and Martha and Delfi, who was part of the family now. They spoke of Morwen too, the sister who Petroc had so nearly lost.

Amos talked to him as he would to a man, not a child, because the things that had happened to him during the last year had not been children's things. His childhood days ended when he had been taken off to serve Carrik, his enemy. Last night he had overcome his fear and been willing to go right into Lord Bellum's castle. Amos would not insult Petroc by treating him as a child.

High Hill was shrouded in mist and the grass was wet with dew. They sat down in a place where on a clear day they would have been able to see most of the island of Karensa. Today, swirling white tendrils obscured their view beyond the Dark Forest, even though the sun was trying to break through the clouds.

"Why is the mist always there?" Petroc asked, suddenly curious.

"It is the time of year, of course. You know that in the Time of Gathering we always have misty mornings."

"No, I don't mean that. I mean the mist over the sea. Why can we never see the world beyond the mist?"

Amos shook his head. "No-one really knows why. The King must have a reason for the mist being there."

They sat in silence for a while, each with their own thoughts. Petroc was remembering Luke and Rosie. What was their world really like? He knew it was very different from Karensa. He would like to see it for himself.

As the sun shone brighter and the mist thinned, they saw them; riders on horseback, riders led by Carrik! And they carried flares.

Petroc's heart lurched with anger and with fear. "Uncle Amos, we must get back to the farm! Carrik is set to destroy it again!"

"Yes, we must get back," Amos agreed. "We must get back because Esram and the girls are on their own."

Morwen snuggled down deeper beneath her covering of furs and let her mind wander freely over the events of the day before.

She had thought she would never see this farm again and she would never forget the feeling of being locked in that cold cell with no hope of escape. She had learnt a hard lesson, but being friends with Salvis again made it almost worthwhile; almost.

And Esram, asleep on the other side of the partition with Petroc and Amos – who would ever have thought that Esram would become one of them?

Morwen liked Esram and she knew that he liked her. When they had danced together, he had been so gentle, as he taught her the steps. He was not like Carrik at all, and if he had been cruel to Petroc and Cherry when they were in Bellum's castle, then he had changed now. He had already risked his life to save Petroc at Black Rock Bay. Now he had risked his life to save her.

She could not remember much about what had happened when they got home last night, but she knew that some of their friends were there to meet them and someone had found her some proper clothes to wear.

She recalled how Cherry had help to wash and change and then put her to bed on clean, sweet hay. The green silk gown had been taken away and burnt for they wanted nothing here that belonged to Bellum's house. New clothes had been found for Esram, too, and his silver tunic ended its days with the green gown on a bonfire in the yard.

Morwen tried to get up quietly but she woke Cherry and that woke Esram and soon they were all up and about.

Amos and Petroc were missing so Morwen decided she would start making breakfast. Cherry went to draw fresh milk from the goat and Morwen began to make a huge bowl of creamy porridge by soaking the oats in water.

Esram had no experience of cooking, so for today he watched what Morwen was doing so that he could learn.

"How do you feel?" she asked.

Esram shook his head. "I don't know. Yesterday I was a lord in a castle. Now I'm a farm boy who has never worked on a farm."

"But you do want to follow the King?"

"Oh yes! But who is there to believe me? I shall always be hated by your people as the King's enemy."

"It will take a long while," Morwen agreed. "But in time people will know you and believe that – what is that noise?"

Cherry hurtled in from the yard. "It's Carrik! Carrik is here! He is coming with soldiers to the farm!"

They all rushed outside and as always it was Morwen who was the practical one.

"Esram, you must hide. It will be you they have come for. We will stay here to meet them. Oh, where are Petroc and Amos?"

Esram did as he was told and the two girls clung tightly together as the riders lined up in the yard. There was no doubt as to what they intended to do.

Morwen and Cherry were desperately afraid, but they tried not to show their fear. What could two young girls do against a group of armed men?

Carrik called to them. "So, you find the farm life more attractive than a castle, Morwen? Well, I do not care about that, it is your choice and you will suffer for it, but where is Esram? Where is my nephew? What have you done to him?"

"Nothing at all, Uncle Carrik." Esram came out of hiding. "I came of my own free will. I am a follower of the King and Salvis now."

Carrik sneered. "Then you will be a follower of Salvis with no roof over your head, for this one is about to go up in flames." He laughed loudly. "Was it hard work rebuilding it, Morwen? You shouldn't have bothered. It will be gone again soon. Was it worth it?"

"Wait!" Amos cut across Carrik as he and Petroc ran across the yard. "I will not let you do this, Carrik! This farm belongs to my sister, Martha, and her family now."

"No, Uncle." Morwen remembered how Tobias had died defending the farm. She would not see her uncle suffer the same end. To her, the farm was not worth such a high price.

Petroc did not agree. Once before, he had sacrificed himself for his friend Luke. Now he did the same thing for his father's farm.

"It is me who Bellum wants," he said resolutely. He placed himself in front of Carrik's horse. "He wants me to go back to him of my own free will. Leave the farm alone and leave the girls alone. I promise I will return with you and shall not try to escape, ever. You will be in favour with Bellum for the rest of your days. Take me, Carrik, and leave the farm. Bellum shall have what he desires."

His face was very white as he dropped to his knees before the hated Carrik.

This was the last thing Carrik had expected. He hesitated, and in that split second, with a mighty crash of thunder, the sky was plunged into darkness.

After the thunder came lightning and with the lightning came rain, but such rain as they had never seen before. At once, the flares they had brought to set fire to the farm were extinguished by the torrent. The yard became mud beneath their feet.

There was more thunder and in this thunder it seemed that a voice spoke, a voice that held all the fury of creation, just as had the wind, the day Bellum lost his crown in the Meadow of Flowers.

The children clung to Amos in fear as rain splashed from the roof and water streamed across the land. This was no ordinary storm. It was a storm commanded by the King himself in his anger.

Carrik's men fled, their horses neighing wildly. Then, as suddenly as it had begun, the storm ceased and daylight returned.

Carrik's eyes were glazed with fear as his horse threw him and fled, leaving him crawling on his knees in the mud.

They watched, first in horror then in amazement as his hands clawed the soft ground. His eyes were rolling wildly. Suddenly, he threw himself full length in the mud.

"This King really is King!" he shouted. "None other could command the wind and rain! Salvis really is the King's son! He is Lord! There is none other like you, Salvis! Forgive me, Lord! I have turned from you in so many ways! I have persecuted your followers! Be my Lord! I turn away from Bellum and all he stands for!"

The King's son heard him from his home in the Royal Palace. The sun came out. The heat made clouds of steam rise from their wet clothes.

"Who the Son sets free, is free indeed," said Morwen.

Chapter 18

Butterfly Song

News of the strange storm quickly spread and very soon all their friends came to the farmhouse to find out what had really happened.

When they heard how the King had saved the farm from being burnt down by sending such rain, and how Carrik had forsaken Bellum to follow Salvis, they wanted to meet together to praise their mighty King.

So, just as they had met many times before, they gathered in Petroc's house to give thanks. Many were uneasy about Carrik and Esram, finding it hard to believe that they could really trust them after all the bad things they had done, and so these two sat alone in a corner of the room while the others sang songs of praise to Salvis and to his father, the King.

Today was unlike the other times. Today, as their songs rose up, they all became very aware of Salvis himself being with them. They could not see him, but each person felt his love flow through them and over them.

Only one thing spoilt Morwen's happiness today; Petroc still refused to believe. He was gracious enough not to stop them from using his house for their meeting, yet he sat by Morwen's side like a lump of stone, refusing to join in the singing.

He seemed very unhappy about the way things were going as the sense of the King's son being with them grew stronger and stronger with each song of praise.

Morwen looked at Cherry, but Cherry was so lost in thinking about Salvis that she did not notice. A strange thought came into Morwen's mind. It did not come from her. She believed Salvis may have put it there.

She slipped from her place and tip-toed up to Amos and Raldi, who were leading the meeting.

Amos bent his head so Morwen could whisper in his ear.

"Uncle Amos, I think Salvis wants to heal Cherry's foot."

The two men looked at each other and then back to her.

"It is a long way to the King's Palace," Amos whispered doubtfully. "We cannot go today. Perhaps another time?"

"No, I believe Salvis wants to heal her and we do not have to go to the King's Palace." Morwen was becoming agitated.

Raldi saw how she was feeling.

He said, "The maiden could be right. We cannot ignore this. What shall we do?"

"I know what to do," Morwen said quickly. "I saw Salvis do it many times when we were all living at the Bay of Dolphins. Please let me try."

"Is it what you really feel, child?" Amos asked kindly.

"Yes," she nodded. "I can feel Salvis speaking into my heart."

"She should try," Raldi decided and he called Cherry out to the front.

Cherry looked worried. "What have I done?" she asked as she stood before the whole company.

Morwen smiled, feeling a sudden rush of compassion for her, How could she ever have been jealous? The thought of it was shameful.

She told Cherry what she felt Salvis wanted to do.

"Would you let me try? Are you willing?" she asked.

Cherry began to tremble. "I do want Salvis to make me better. What do I have to do?"

"Nothing," Morwen told her, remembering how Salvis had done this in the past. "You never knew Salvis like we did, but think about him now. Think about how gentle and kind he is."

"All right then. I am willing."

Cherry closed her eyes and Morwen knelt down and placed her hands on the damaged foot. There was a sudden hush in the room as everyone supported Morwen by silently asking the King for Cherry to be healed.

"Please, Lord King," Morwen began. "Please make this foot well again. We don't want Cherry to hurt any more." Then she grew more confident. "Lord King, I know you healed people through Salvis and you gave us the same power. Show us how to use it like Salvis did. Heal her now, Lord, please."

"Is that it?" Cherry asked, feeling embarrassed and glad that it was over. Her foot was very warm.

Morwen was disappointed that nothing seemed to have happened. How could she ever have thought that she could do the work of Salvis? Who did she think she was?

As Cherry moved to go back to her seat, a cry arose from the assembly. The limp had gone!

Cherry began to laugh and cry at the same time.

"It doesn't hurt any more! I can walk as well as you now! Morwen, you have done it! Thank you!"

"Not me," said Morwen hastily. "Thank the King, not me, Cherry. He made you well. All I did was to ask."

Then she too began to cry, but this time it was with joy. It was true! They did have the King's power.

Everyone began to praise the King saying how great he was and thanking him for sending his son, Salvis, to rescue the people of Karensa. They praised him as never before.

Except for Petroc; Petroc walked out of the room.

****

Morwen followed him. He was walking so fast that she had to run to keep up with him and it was like that all the way to High Hill, to the very spot where he had sat with Amos that morning.

Morwen struggled to get her breath.

"Petroc, why do you hate Salvis?" she panted. "You were always loyal to the King."

"I don't hate the King," Petroc replied, staring straight ahead cross the sea.

"Then why won't you accept that Salvis is his son and Lord of Karensa and ask him to fill you with his love and power?"

"Oh Salvis, Salvis! If it is not the King, it is Salvis! Salvis is dead. I saw him die in Bellum's stronghold. It was his ghost we saw later on the beach."

"It was not a ghost. You sat and talked to him. He lifted me in his arms. A ghost could not do that. He was real."

"Then where is he now?"

"You know where, back in the King's Palace. That is why the King sent the new power to us. Oh, Petroc, please, why will you not ask him to be lord of your life?"

"I did that when he talked to me on the beach, but nothing happened!" her brother shouted angrily. He had never told anyone that before.

Morwen was lost for words. Salvis would never refuse anyone. Something must be wrong.

"Maybe you did not ask properly," she said lamely.

All at once, Petroc understood. He had asked Salvis into his life many times, but it had always been on his own terms. He had not been willing for Salvis to change any part of his life.

He had not allowed him to take away his anger and hatred and he had not been willing to forgive Carrik or even Esram. He still wanted to hate the people who had hurt him.

He had to let go of his hatred, even of the man who had killed his father. Salvis had no room in his own heart for hatred and he expected those who would follow him to forgive, just as he did.

To his dismay, tears streamed down his face as he acknowledged his hardness of heart. His father would not be pleased with his efforts to rebuild the farm because he had done it for the wrong reasons.

In a torrent of love and shame, the hatred left him and was gone for ever, swept away by the immense love of the King's son.

"Lord, please forgive me. Help me to forgive and forget the hurt. Be my lord for ever."

"Petroc," Morwen whispered through her own tears. "Petroc, he is here. Lord Salvis is here."

And this time he really was there.

He was standing behind them by a clump of yellow gorse and he looked just as he had looked the last time they had seen him on the beach. His kind, brown eyes were still so full of love for them.

"Petroc, it has been such a long time," he said gently.

Petroc and Morwen fell to their knees before him. It felt like the right place to be.

"I cannot stay long with you," he told them. "As you see me now, is not really how I am. If I were to appear to you as I really am, your hearts would fail you. My true place now is in the King's Palace at my father's side. I have come because I have things I delight to tell you. Come, sit with me and listen; listen well."

The children sat on the hillside with Salvis and they listened carefully as the King's son continued to speak to them in that same gentle voice, sharing secrets with them never before shared. Brother and sister lost track of time as they listened intently.

"And finally," said Salvis, "I have work for you to do. Petroc, the King has a purpose for your farm. You are to make it a special place where all those who follow me, rich or poor, are always made welcome."

"Yes, Lord, it will be so."

"For Carrik and Esram I have other work. Let them stay with you for a while and learn about me, and when they have learnt, they must go to reach the people on the far side of the island. These people do not really understand why I came. You must be sure to tell Carrik this."

Again, Petroc was curious about other lands.

"Salvis," he said, "what about the world beyond the mist? What about Luke's world? Do the people there know about you?"

"In that world," Salvis replied, "one innocent Man gave up his own life to pay the price for those who are guilty. This Man now lives forever and anyone who is really sorry can turn to him and be forgiven. He is the Son of the Greatest King Ever, and this true story is told in a very special book called the Bible."

Petroc was pleased that Luke and Rosie were not alone in the world beyond the mist.

"What about me, Lord Salvis?" Morwen murmured. "I know I was foolish and turned away from you, but I never will again."

"Morwen, you are dear to me. You of all people understand me. You were foolish and listened to Bellum when he whispered wrong thoughts in your ear. Learn from it, my child. You found it easy to enter the Castle of Shadows but only the King could get you out."

"Yes, Lord, I have learnt that. I will not go back again."

"Do not make rash promises, child. Learn how to live in the King's power as you have done today when the King healed your friend's foot. Let your heart become gentle again as it was long ago. And do not look so upset, for you will learn and then the King has work for you to do. Until then, live under your brother's authority. Help him and give him your support.

"You, Petroc, be kind to your sister as you were in the days before the war. You must both help Esram too, and Cherry."

Morwen's cheeks burned as she remembered her jealousy.

"Petroc, you once wanted to touch me to make sure I was alive. Do so now," Salvis offered.

"Lord... I... I cannot!" Petroc exclaimed. "I want to believe without touching you."

"Well done. Now, I must leave you, but you shall see me again. One day you will come to live with me in the King's Palace but until then my thoughts are always close to you."

He placed his hands above each of their heads in turn and then he was gone.

Morwen opened her eyes to see Petroc smiling down at her and once more he was the brother she loved.

They stood together, brother and sister at peace with each other after such a long time.

"So much has happened in a year, Petroc," Morwen sighed.

"So much has happened since we met Luke and Rosie. Look at the mist, Morwen. Does it never move?"

"Once it did, when you were not here. There is a land not far away, a land where Luke and Rosie live."

"Perhaps we shall see them again soon."

"I hope so." Morwen linked her arm to his. "We have so much to tell them."

"I want to tell Luke about meeting Salvis today." Petroc's voice was filled with awe.

From this moment on, no matter what happened to him in his life, whether good or bad, if he should prosper or if he should die, there would never be another day like this day, for on this day the King's own son had come to him and forgiven him and made him his own.

As they stood together, the butterflies returned and flocked around them.

"It's as though Salvis told them to come and thank you for setting them free from the Castle of Shadows."

Morwen began to sing in words older than time and sweeter than tomorrow's dawn, secret words of ancient days, words of power and great beauty. Soon, Petroc joined in.

The notes rose and fell and rose again on the breeze, and mingled with the gentle song of the butterflies.

THE END OF THE BEGINNING

Lightning Source UK Ltd.
Milton Keynes UK
05 May 2010
153731UK00001B/13/P